Super Pencil

&

The Revenge of the Talking Televisions

Eugene L. Gatewood

Created by Micah E. Gatewood

© 2018 Eugene L. Gatewood

All rights reserved.

ISBN: 0692965386

ISBN 13: 9780692965382

Library of Congress Control Number: 2018903461

LCCN Imprint Name: Aurora, IL

Dedication

To my big homie: Your innocence and imagination inspires me in more ways than you will ever know. You ignited something inside of me that caused us to create something that will impact generations. Thank you for expanding and enhancing my legacy. I love you, son!

To my wife: You are a true helpmate, friend, and partner. There is no one with whom I would prefer to take this journey called life. Thank you for reminding me that I am a Difference Maker. W.E.3

Contents

Chapter 1: Meet Jeff Whitman 5

Chapter 2: Jeff Meets Billy 11

Chapter 3: Jeff Meets Phil (and Hines Redgrave) 23

Chapter 4: Hines's Plotting Begins 53

Chapter 5: Jeff's Big "Date" 64

Chapter 6: The Revenge of the Talking Televisions 78

Chapter 7: Summer Time Is Coming 93

Chapter 8: Super Pencil! 100

Chapter 9: Jeff Meets Joel 108

Chapter 10: The Plot Thickens 116

Chapter 11: Don't Worry, Be Happy! 131

Chapter 12: Jeff's New Squad 147

Chapter 13: The Big Payback 160

Chapter 14: A New School Year 166

Chapter 1

Meet Jeff Whitman

"Take that!" Jeff blurted as the action figures in each of his hands collided with one another. "Is that all you have got? You will never stop me from destroying the entire world!" Jeff lunged from one side of the room to the other, passing the window of his bedroom. The sunlight beat against his mocha skin and caused him to squint as it pierced his large brown eyes. The commotion got the attention of Jeff's dad who was outside in the driveway preparing to wash his car. It was a pleasant summer morning. The sun illuminated the sky and heated the air. The occasional wind whisked through the leaves of the trees and provided an undertone to the birds chirping. Illinois weather was unpredictable, so Mr. Whitman wanted to make the best of it by completing a few outdoor chores. Jeff's bedroom window was slightly open. The morning breeze caused the curtains in Jeff's bedroom to move rhythmically to the music Jeff was listening to. "Is that Michael Jackson?" Jeff's father looked up toward Jeff's bedroom window, shook his head, and smiled. The song made him reminisce about being Jeff's age. Musics from the 1980's and 1990's were Jeff's favorite. "How does he find these songs?" Mr. Whitman continued to shake his head in disbelief as he turned his attention back to the hood of his car. Jeff loved most things retro, especially his music. As Mr. Whitman made circular strokes on the hood of his car to reveal the showroom shine, he could hear the mumble of Jeff's voice above his head. He could make out what Jeff was saying, but as Jeff leaped back to the other side of his room, with his arms high above his head, he knew he was locked into an epic battle with his action figures. "Crash!" The loud noise caused Mr. Whitman head to jerk toward Jeff's bedroom window. "Jeff, are you ok? What are you doing up there?"

Jeff stood motionless in the middle of his room. The deep tone of his dad calling his name always seemed to paralyze him instantly.

"I'm ok; nothing to see here. Keep it moving!" Jeff replied as he picked up his basketball trophies that had fallen like dominos when he bumped into his book self. Jeff Whitman was your average rough-and-tumble boy. He was taller that most kids but had a slender frame. He was active in many sports, but basketball was his favorite. He liked to wrestle and loved listening to music. Michael Jackson was his favorite artist. Although he enjoyed music from the 80's and 90's, his clothing was more trendy and fashionable. Jeff had to "stay fly" as he called it. Getting a fresh cut was important to Jeff. Going to the barbershop with his dad was something that he always looked forward to. Besides, he learned a lot of cool stuff in the barbershop. That's where he got all of his ideas about what shoes to buy, clothes to wear, and cool phrases to say. Jeff did not always understand what they talked about, but the barbershop was not just a visit; it was an experience.

Jeff had another passion; he had an incredible imagination. Writing stories and creating comic-book characters brought Jeff so much joy. Pretending to "save the world" as an action hero was Jeff's favorite pastime. Jeff's imagination allowed him to escape any environment. He did not even need action figures. Jeff would use whatever he had access to at the time: a pencil, a marker, or a few random Legos that lay around. No matter the object, his mind could create an epic adventure out of anything! After fighting off the evil villain, Jeff grabbed his pencil and notepad to log how he had just saved the world with his action figures.

Jeff also dreamed of being famous one day. He would daydream about his name being in bright lights, and being on a big stage, or making the game-winning shot at the buzzer with fans calling his name. That made him excited. Last year, Jeff's grandmother (he calls her Granna) bought him a basketball hoop for Christmas. He worked hard practicing to perfect his killer crossover and step-back jump shot. He could not wait to try it out on a few of his friends. However, when Jeff played outside, often he played alone. Being an only child, he had gotten used to playing by himself. He was OK with playing alone, but he really enjoyed the company of others. During the school year, Jeff had plenty of classmates to play with. However, he did not have many friends to hang out with once he got home. He often daydreamed about a big, evil super blob that swallowed all of the kids as they walked home from school; after all, how come he never saw them outside playing? Being the only African- American student in his class, one of the few in his school, and the only one who lived on his street, crossed his mind periodically. Jeff never mentioned to his parents that it crossed his mind sometimes. Besides, he did not know how he felt about it. He simply noticed it. Mr. and Mrs. Whitman searched for school systems they thought would prepare Jeff for success. They considered the racial mix of each suburb while preparing to purchase a home. Although the percentage of African-American students was low in the one they chose, the school district was diverse. They had not discussed the school's diversity with Jeff. They wanted him to make friends and assimilate without creating a bias. However, it became apparent that Jeff realized he was different when Mr. Whitman chaperoned a field trip. As they walked around a museum, an old classroom photo was on display. Within the photo there was one African-American boy with twenty-two white classmates. "Dad look! He is the only dark skinned kid just like me!" Mr. Whitman made eye contact with Jeff's teacher whose eyes had widened as she released a slight gasp. Mr. Whitman paused to observe how his teacher would respond. "You are very observant Jeff," his teacher replied as they continued to walk to the next exhibit. "Good recovery." Jeff's dad nodded his head with a slight grin. Although, Mr. Whitman knew he would have to talk to his wife to come up with a plan for talking about diversity with Jeff later.

One blissful summer afternoon, the sound of the bouncing basketball and swish of the nets permeated the block. Jeff was working on his crossover and a jump shot in his driveway. "Why don't other kids like playing outside as much as I do?" Jeff wondered. "Where are all of the other kids?" Jeff looked down his street in both directions after taking another shot.

Gnats circled Jeff's head and buzzed around his ears, nose, and mouth with every shot he took. "Ugh!" Jeff gasped. "Ewww, a bug just flew into my mouth!" Jeff spat it out with disgust. After the second bug flew up Jeff's nose, he was done. "It's time to go inside."

Watching movies on his dad's "secret TV" is what Jeff did while indoors. He called it the secret TV because it was hidden behind a large painting that hung on their living room wall. The painting covered a large shelf that was embedded into the wall. As Jeff's dad removed the painting from the wall, Jeff asked, "What kind of TV used to fit into a space again?" "TVs were not always thin like they are now. Back when I was younger, televisions were big, boxy, clunky, and extremely heavy." Jeff remembered seeing a television like that at his Granna's house.

"Oh, so you are talking about the TVs from back in the day, like in the 1900's?"

"1900's? I am not that old!" Mr. Whitman recoiled. "Well, I guess you are technically correct. It was the 1900's or early 2000's." he continued as he thought over what Jeff said.

Super Pencil & The Revenge of the Talking Televisions

As days passed, Jeff's parents noticed that he watched the secret TV more and more instead of playing outside.

"It's nice out. Why are you inside?" Jeff's mom asked.

"No reason," Jeff replied. "Just gonna watch some TV."

It was out of character for Jeff to play indoors given how much he enjoyed playing outside, but his parents allowed their suspicions to pass.

Chapter 2

Jeff Meets Billy

After several days in a row of Jeff staying inside, Jeff's dad invited him to go outside for a game of one-on-one. Jeff was super competitive and did not like to lose. Jeff's dad was competitive as well and would not allow Jeff to win. "11-2! Point game. What's wrong? Are you giving up? We don't...." Losing to his dad made Jeff really frustrated. He dreamed of beating him one day, so he practiced and played harder every time, and his skills improved.

"One day I will be taller, stronger, and faster, and I will dunk over your head!" Jeff mumbled after his dad scored the winning jump shot.

"One day, son. Keep practicing, and one day that may come true. But today..." Jeff's dad taunted Jeff with his arm still extended above his head, jiggling his fingers.

Later that night, after dinner, Jeff and his mom and dad walked to the ice cream shop that was near their home. Jeff called it "3 Flavors" because the three of them always picked the same flavors. Jeff got a scoop of vanilla on a cake cone, with rainbow sprinkles. His mom loved to get a scoop of chocolate inside a waffle cone, and Jeff's dad would always get a scoop of chocolate chip cookie dough in a cup.

The sun had begun to set, but it was still hot and steamy outside. Jeff held the door open for a shorter kid and who appeared to be his little sister and parents, who followed behind him exiting 3 Flavors. As Jeff tried to quickly read what was on the boys graphic T-shirt, he did not realize that he had tilted his cone to the side while holding the door. At the last second, Jeff released the door with his left hand and caught the scoop before it fell from the cone.

"Whew. That was close!" Jeff sighed.

"Here are some napkins." The kid he'd held the door for offered Jeff one of his napkins giving him a shy look.

"Thank you, sir!" Jeff replied.

"Sir? I am only ten years old," the boy responded. His light brown eyes shot over to his mom for an explanation.

"He is just being polite, Billy," his mom chimed in.

"Hi, my name is Jeff Whitman. Nice to meet you, Billy." Jeff extended his right hand to shake Billy's. The ice cream was still dripping from Jeff's hand, so Billy just handed him more napkins.

"How does he know my name?" Billy thought as he looked at his mom and dad for further explanation.

"Thanks for the napkins," Jeff said with a grin.

"No problem —sir?" Billy answered sheepishly. Jeff chuckled, which made Billy laugh.

Jeff and Billy continued to talk outside of 3 Flavors. Jeff learned that he and Billy were both 10 years old and would be attending The Wheatland's Elementary School in the fall. Jeff's parents introduced themselves and Mr. and Mrs. Ramirez returned the pleasantries. They made small talk outside of the ice cream shop while the boys became more acquainted. Billy's family had recently moved to the neighborhood.

"We live a few blocks over on Oakfield Court," Mrs. Ramirez explained.

"Wait, we live on the same street?" Mr. Whitman replied.

"Wow! Really? But I have never seen you outside playing!" Jeff said after he overheard Mrs. Ramirez say what street they lived on.

Billy's dad interjected with frustration in his voice, "We tell Billy all the time: you will never make new friends in the house playing video games all day!"

The small talk continued. Everyone was eating his or her ice cream really fast to keep it from melting in the heat.

"It was great meeting you. I am sure we will see you around," Mrs. Whitman said to Mrs. Ramirez. Jeff and his family said their goodbyes and began to walk home as Billy's family got into their car and drove away.

"They were a nice family!" Jeff's dad expressed.

"Yeah, Billy is a nice kid," Jeff replied. As they walked home, Jeff pondered, "I wonder why I have never seen him playing outside?"

A couple of days later, Jeff was playing basketball in his driveway. He forgot to remove his superhero cap that he often wore when writing comic books. Being in character helped spark his imagination while writing or acting out a scene. His superhero cape flapped in the wind as he jumped toward the basket to make a layup. As he grabbed the rebound, he saw a boy and a little girl a few houses down. The boy looked a lot like Billy, the kid he'd met at the ice cream shop. His dad was working in the garage, so he asked him if he could go down the street to see if it was Billy.

"Hi Billy!" Jeff shouted as he got closer and realized it was indeed him.

"Jeff! What are you doing here?"

"I live right down there!" Jeff turned and pointed back toward his house. "But I've never seen you outside when I'm outside playing." Jeff was panting to catch his breath running down the street and trying to maintain his excitement.

"Yeah, my mom and dad tell me to go outside more, but..."

"Want to come shoot some hoops with me?" Jeff interrupted excitedly.

Billy looked at his mom and dad for approval, and they nodded to assure him it was OK. "Why do you have that cape on?" Billy asked.

"It's for saving the world!" Jeff replied as he bolted back toward his driveway. The flare of the cape hit Billy in the face causing his dark brown hair to uncover his right eye. Mr. Ramirez grabbed the grocery bags from Billy's hands while Mrs. Ramirez slight nudged Billy forward in the small of his back. Billy took off on a slight jog to catch up with Jeff. Billy quickly glanced back one more time as he caught up with Jeff to see if his parents were still watching.

Mr. and Mrs. Ramirez were extremely happy that Jeff came down to talk to Billy. Since Billy was new to the neighborhood, his parents were concerned about him having a hard time making new friends once school began. They moved around a lot because of Mr. Ramirez's job. He was an executive at a telecommunications company. At Billy's previous schools, recess had become really stressful for him. All of the other kids played with classmates they knew from prior years or around their neighborhood. It was difficult for Billy to work up enough courage to ask his classmates if he could play with them, so Billy reconnecting with Jeff after their encounter at the ice cream shop was a huge relief for both Billy and his parents.

Jeff and Billy played together outside more and more for the rest of the summer. "Billy! If you are going to be outside, please come in and put on sunscreen." Mrs. Ramirez cracked the inner door to the garage and yelled out to Billy. She was always concerned about his beige skin tone being protected from the sun. "Want to go inside and play video games or something?" Billy suggested to prevent him from having to put on sunscreen. But Jeff was so excited and engrossed in "saving the world" that he did not hear Billy dropping hints that he wanted to go inside.

One day, Jeff showed Billy all of the comics he had drawn. "Which one do you want to act out next?" Jeff asked Billy. Billy stared blankly at what seemed to be hundreds of comics.

"Chicken Man! What is that?" Billy said while looking away to hide his smile because he did not want to make Jeff feel embarrassed.

"Oh, that is story about a half chicken half human who flies around the world saving all of the animals who are in danger of becoming extinct because of the humans."

"How do you come up with this stuff?" It inspired Billy to learn that Jeff liked animals too. He really liked cats. He had two pet cats at home, Felix and Oscar. Billy continued to thumb through all of the titles

"I was watching a YouTube video about how chickens are killed so that we can eat them. It made me kinda sad. So, I wanted to save all of the animals that are hurt by humans."

Billy paused as he processed the fact that we have to kill animals to have food to eat. Distracted by the realization, Billy made a mental note to talk to his parents about that later. He grabbed two of the action figures that were lying on the floor. "Look! There is a cat caught in the tree. Looks like a job for Chicken Man!" Billy's voice deepened as he got into character and then he paused. "Wait, chickens can't fly?"

"I know silly! But in our world, anything is possible!" Jeff exclaimed as they both laughed and used their action figures to climb the bookshelf that had become an imaginary large tree. Billy looked out his window and could see the large trees in front of his house. He began to imagine what he would do if his cats got stuck in those trees. He needed to practice climbing them.

"Jeff, let's go out and practice climbing the trees in front of my house." Billy walked toward the window and pulled back the curtains and sheers so that he could see more clearly. Jeff walked to the window. The thought of climbing an actual tree had never crossed Jeff's mind before, but the adrenaline rush made Billy's request hard to resist.

"Looks like a job for Chicken Man!" Jeff's right eyebrow rose as he strapped on his cap and placed his hands on his hips. Jeff tilted his head up and to the side and posed as if he was on the cover of a comic book. This caused Billy to burst out in laughter and Jeff did the same.

Jeff made Billy a cape out of an old pillowcase so that they could climb the trees and save the world together. Jeff was excited to have a new friend to hang out with, and Billy eventually enjoyed reading comic books and pretending to save the world. Although, he really did still enjoy playing video games inside. he wanted Jeff to come to his house sometimes, but enjoyed hanging out with Jeff so much, he did not want to do anything that would jeopardize it.

As the days went by, kids looked out of their windows and saw Jeff and Billy with their capes, running, climbing trees, jumping off the porch, and diving over the bushes, so they decided to come out to see what they were doing. "We are saving the world!" Jeff would exclaim each time a new kid asked him. Each day, more kids came outside to join in on all of the fun that Jeff and Billy were having. Some days they played basketball, other days they rode bikes or had water-gun fights, but for Jeff, nothing compared to the days they all wore costumes, pretending to save the world. The porches and windows were lined with parents with phones in hand, recording video and taking pictures of how creative their children were being. It had become a summer that Jeff had dreamed of.

On the other hand, for Billy, he actually missed playing video games. Every morning, Jeff would come ring the doorbell to see if Billy could come out and play. Although Billy loved to hang out with Jeff, it impeded on the times he was allowed to play video games.

"Ding Dong!" the sound of the doorbell echoed through the house.

"Mijo! Answer the door. We are sure it is Jeff coming to see you." Mrs. Ramirez called out from her bedroom. After a few moments the doorbell rang again, but she did not hear the little pitter patter of Billy's footsteps running down the stairs to greet Jeff. She jumped up to see him still sitting on the bed looking sad. She ran down stairs and opened the door just as Jeff was bouncing his basketball down the drive way.

"Oh, hi Mrs. Ramirez. Can Billy come out to play?"

"Billy is not available right now. I will have him come down later." Mrs. Ramirez said as she smiled and waved to Jeff. She walked into Billy's bedroom and he looked out the window watching Jeff sprint down the sidewalk while dribbling the basketball. The faint sound of the ball bouncing was audible.

"Mijo, is everything ok? Why do you look so said? What happened between you and Jeff?" Mrs. Ramirez was concerned.

"No. Everything is fine."

"Is he started to be mean like the other kids used to?"

"No mom. Jeff is always nice to me."

"Then I don't understand. Why did you avoid him today?"

"I mean, we always do what he wants to do. But we never come to my house to do things that I like."

"Have you asked him to come over?"

"Well, once." Billy glanced up and to the left trying to remember if he had asked any other times.

"What did he say when you asked him?"

"He said yes and we came down and climbed the tree to save Felix and Oscar."

"Oh no, how did they get out? I did not know they were stuck in the tree. You never told your dad or me."

"No Madre! We were playing Chicken Man, so I had to practice climbing the tree just in case."

"Chicken Man?" Mrs. Ramirez thought but did not have a chance to ask, because Billy continued to talk and she did not want to interrupt him.

"Jeff is one of the best friends I have ever had, but I would just like to do stuff that I like sometimes. I never see him playing video games."

"Mijo, maybe you have to just ask him. He will never know that you like to do other things like soccer, playing at the playground, and riding your bike if you never tell him. Maybe he likes doing those things too. Does Jeff have a bike?"

"Yeah he does." Billy paused and started to get excited about the potential of going bike riding. "Can I ride my bike?"

"Maybe you can see if Jeff wants to ride bikes up to the park together?"

"What if he says no?" Billy's eyes closed slightly as his head angled downward.

"You will never know until you ask."

Billy looked out the window to see if Jeff was still outside. He wanted to hurry so that he would not miss a chance to hang out with his buddy. As he pulled his bike out of the garage, Jeff saw him riding down the driveway and toward him on the sidewalk.

"What's up Billy?"

"Hey Jeff! You wanna ride up to the park and hang out?" Billy's words seem to suck all of the salivae from his mouth as he spoke them. "He's going to say no. Please don't say no." Billy thought as Jeff turned away to look in the garage.

"Hey dad! Can you take my bike down off the rack? Billy and I are going to the park."

"Yes!" Billy sighed in relief. Billy's mom spied from his bedroom window. Her arms shot toward the ceiling with both fists clenched tightly as she observed Mr. Whitman roll Jeff's bike from the garage. Billy glanced back toward the house and the joy in his brown eye's brought tears to hers. Because they moved around so much, she and Mr. Ramirez felt guilty about how it prevented Billy from developing lasting friendships with kids his age. He had family members his age, but the distance prevented them from growing up together. Jeff was the longest running friendship that Billy has had to date. This made her very happy. She anxiously watched as they rode next to one another, wobbling back and forth nearly colliding with every rotation of the pedal.

Chapter 3

Jeff Meets Phil (and Hines Redgrave)

P hil Parker was one of Jeff's best friends even though they had never been in the same class. Jeff and Phil first met several years ago during the summer before third grade. They attended a summer camp at the local community center. They had so much in common. They went to the same school, liked to play sports, and most of all, they both loved to read comic books and then pretend to save the world. Occasionally their parents would get them together to hang out, but not as often as they would've liked to. Phil lived a few subdivisions away, so they had to depend on their parents to plan when they got together. Because of the distance their parents did not allow them to walk or ride bikes to each other's homes. In the summertime, it was extremely frustrating that they rarely saw each other outside of summer camp, especially when Redgrave was around. Well, speaking of Hines, let's first see how he and Phil became friends.

Meet Hines Redgrave and Phil Parker

When Jeff met Phil, he already had a best friend named Hines Redgrave. Hines was much taller and heavier than most kids their age, so many of them felt intimidated by his size. He had sandy brown hair and his face had a reddish tint due to the freckles that spotted his cheeks and nose. His loud raspy voice frequently echoed down the hallways distracting the kids who sat at their desks at each classroom. Every student would watch the window next to his or her classroom door; listening for what vulgar word Hines might spray into the atmosphere.

"Eye's on me! Worry about yourself!" Mr. Goldberg clapped his hands so hard that it startled Jeff and his classmates.

Phil and Hines had been in the same class since kindergarten. It always made him concerned for Hines when he left the classroom in that way. They played at each other's homes during the school year and almost daily throughout the summer. Phil and Hines became really close while in first grade. Hines and his dad had a great relationship. Mr. Redgrave called Hines his best friend. Hines's dad was in the military. Mr. Redgrave was deployed to the Middle East the summer before Hines went into first grade. Hines was having a hard time because he really missed his dad. They used to spend so much time together. Mr. Redgrave took Hines to several Blackhawk games. This was when Hines developed his love for hockey. Mr. Redgrave taught Hines how to ice skate when he was just four years old. Hines seemed to be a natural because he picked up on skating so quickly. Shortly thereafter, his dad purchased him a hockey stick, roller blades, and a goal. They would play hockey in the driveway almost every day.

"Hines, it's time for dinner honey." Mrs. Redgrave cracked the screen door beckoning Hines to come in to eat.

"No. Dad will be here in a minute and we are gonna play hockey." Hines leaned forward with every engine roar and tire hum that came down his street. His dad was dropped off in a different car every day, depending on which one of his co-workers brought him home from work.

"Finally!" Hines said as he bounced to his feet and shot the puck toward the net while his dad tried to stop it as he jumped out of the car. They played for a few moments, but Hines could tell that his dad was not into it like other days.

"Time to go in. It's gettin' dark. You eaten yet?" Mr. Redgrave asked. "Not yet." Hines replied as he took one last shot. "Go get washed up. I will call you down when dinner is ready." Mr. Redgrave scooped up his coat and went through the front door as Hines entered the house through the garage.

"I got the call today. I am being deployed to the Middle East again." Mr. Redgrave told his wife as he tossed his coat over the arm of the chair after walking in from playing hockey with Hines.

"Oh my God! When?" Mrs. Redgrave slammed her laptop close and then dropped her head and covered her face with both of her hands.

Mr. Redgrave embraced his wife as tears began to flow down her face. He had been deployed for months in the past. Mrs. Redgrave dreaded the thought of the toil it took on her and Hines every time he was gone.

"How long?" Mrs. Redgrave mumbled through her hands that were still covering her face.

"I am not sure. It could be up to a year, maybe more." Mr. Redgrave turned around as he heard another whimper coming from behind him. It was Hines standing on the threshold of the kitchen. He had heard their entire conversation. Hines turned and ran upstairs to his bedroom and slammed the door.

"Hines! Honey!" Mr. and Mrs. Redgrave followed behind him knocking on his bedroom door with their ear pressed against it. As they stood at the door pleading with Hines to open up, Hines's older brother Luke came home and walked up the stairs.

"What's going on here?" He walked past them thinking his little brother was just having another episode. Although, the timing was odd because it had never happened while his dad was home.

"We need to talk." Mr. Redgrave reached for Luke and gently touched his shoulder to get his attention.

"Whatever it is, I did not do it." Luke turned slightly to brush pass the nudge of Mr. Redgrave. Mr. Redgrave was not Luke's father. His mom had him at a very young age. His father left shortly after he was born. He had met him a couple of times, but they did not have a good relationship. His dad found out he was good with computers and wanted to be an engineer. Therefore, he consistently sent money to pay for classes and camps to help him develop his knowledge and skills, but that was the extent of their relationship. In the beginning, Luke and Mr. Redgrave had a good relationship until Hines was born. Then, it seemed like Hines got all of the attention and Mr. Redgrave no longer had time for him. Luke sometimes envied the relationship that Hines had with his dad, so he did not appreciate the subtly advances Mr. Redgrave made to foster a better relationship with him. His envy also affected his relationship with his brother Hines. It became a competition.

"You take Hines and I will handle him." Mrs. Redgrave walked away and stopped Luke's bedroom door before it slammed shut.

"Hines. Buddy. Open the door." After a few more seconds, Mr. Redgrave heard the click of the door unlocking then gently twisted the knob, entered and sat on the edge of his bed.

"I know it's hard when I have to go away. Daddy has made a commitment to our country, so I have to complete what I started."

"But I miss you when you are away!" Mr. Redgrave pulled Hines closer and wiped his tears.

"I can buy you a dog?"

"I hate dogs! You know I am afraid of them." Hines' voice was muffled against his dad's chest.

"I will call and write you all the time. Just like last time." Mr. Redgrave's words did not comfort Hines at this time. Hines did not have many friends. His dad was the only person that made him feel special and that he belonged. Hines's six-year-old mind could not articulate exactly how he felt. All he knew was that he would miss him. Luke was not as disappointed that Mr. Redgrave was leaving. His mother's focus was more on him whenever Mr. Redgrave was deployed. It was more like old times, before Hines and Mr. Redgrave were in the picture. Given that he was seven years older than Hines, he helped his mother care for little brother while she was at work. Although he did not exactly like to do it, he felt needed by his mother and that gave him comfort.

It was a month into the school year. Mr. Redgrave had been gone for about six weeks. The school had called Mrs. Redgrave each week due to Hines' behavior. During the first week of school, Hines was angry because he could not get a drink of water, so he knocked several trays and pencil holders off Mrs. Davis' desk. Mrs. Davis alerted the Principal, Mrs. Phillips and he came to take Hines to his office. Hines yelled vulgarities as Mrs. Phillips walked him to her office. His loud raspy voice echoed down the hallway distracting the kids who sat at their desks in each classroom. Every student watched the window anticipating a brawny statured reddish blur to stream past his or her classroom at any time. They eagerly listened for what discourteous words that might spray into the atmosphere.

"Eye's on me! Worry about yourself!" Mr. Goldberg clapped his hands so hard that it startled Jeff and his classmates.

A week went by and the school had not called Mrs. Redgrave. She made a mental note to call the school Monday morning to ensure that all was well. During the week, Hines made mention of a kid named Phil every day when he got home from school.

"Who is Phil?" Mrs. Redgrave continued to unload the grocery bags and place items in the pantry.

"He is a kid in my first grade class."

"What do you like about him?"

"He is very nice to me." Hines said as he put the milk in the pantry trying to be helpful. His mother did not say anything about him putting the milk in the pantry. She wanted him to continue to talk about his newfound friend and did not want to distract him with a rebuke.

"Can he come over to play video games with me?" Mrs. Redgrave paused and stared at Hines with her mouth slightly open. Her hesitation caused Hines's shoulders to slouch and then he dropped his head and exited the kitchen.

"Oh, yes! I mean yes. He can come over. Do you know his last name?" This was the first time Hines had ever asked if a friend could come to play. Honestly, she did not think he had many friends left at school. Due to his occasional aggressive behavior, the teachers reported that most kids steered clear of him during recess and lunchtime. Hines would try to engage with other kids as they were playing. They would not reject him, but they did not exactly include him either. Mrs. Redgrave continued to look for the classroom directory hoping that Phil's parents were listed. Hines could not remember Phil's last name, so she hoped there was not more than one child with his name in the class. "Phil Parker!" Her finger stopped on his name as it slid up and down pastel blue sheet of paper. "Laurie Parker. Her cell is listed. Should I call or text?" Mrs. Redgrave paced the floor rehearsing what she would say and how she would start the conversation. "What if Phil is one of the kids that Hines had an incident with in the past month?" She thought. "The school never tells me whom he got into it with. Hines will be crushed if Phil turns down the invite." Mrs. Redgrave decided to text her instead of calling. That way, Hines would not be able to over hear the conversation and she could control how much Hines would know if it did not turn out so well.

"Hi Laurie. You do not know me. I found your number on school's classroom directory. My name is Sherri Redgrave. My son, Hines, talks about your son, Phil, all the time. He asked if I could set up a time for them to play together. Let me know what you think." Mrs. Redgrave read the text multiple times as her thumb hovered over the send button. "Just press it!" she said as she tried to pull back one last time, but it was too late.

"…" the bubble appears immediately. Sherri squirmed in her seat as she gazed at the reply bubbles. Then they disappeared. She stood up quickly with her phone still in her right hand, while extending the fingers on her left hand, palm facing up.

"What happened?" she whispered. The bubbles returned and she took her seat with her eyes still fixed on the phone. Then bubbles disappeared again.

"Ugh!" Sherri watched the phone for several minutes, but the bubbles never returned.

"Mom, I'm hungry." Mrs. Redgrave's head popped up. She did not realize Hines walked back into the kitchen.

"Ok Honey. Dinner will be done shortly." Mrs. Redgrave placed her phone on the kitchen table and started to make dinner for her sons. After dinner, she was loading the dishwasher and saw the screen of her phone illuminating out of the corner of her eye. She pressed her knee and thigh against the door of dishwasher to close it while reaching for her phone. It was a reply from Laurie.

"Hi Sherri. It was very nice of you to reach out. Phil talks about Hines all the time…"

"In a good way or a bad way?" Sherri tried to interpret the tone of the text before finishing reading it. "Just keep reading Sherri!" she said to herself.

"…Phil would love to hang out with Hines." Sherri started running in place and spinning around in the middle of the kitchen. Breathing heavily, she sat down to regain her composure. Her eyesight was slightly blurred, so it took her a second to refocus on the words in the text.

"Actually, Phil and I go to the park every Saturday morning. Perhaps you all can meet us there at 11am. It's the big park off of Route 30. If not tomorrow, we can think of another date and time. Let me know."

Sherri was so excited about the news that she ran upstairs to tell Hines all about it. In her excitement, she did not realize that she never replied to the text from Laurie to confirm that they were coming. The next morning, Hines was up early and ready to go. Mrs. Redgrave had only seen Hines this excited on the days he video called his dad. "Do I have to go?" Luke pleaded to stay at home. "Yes!" We are leaving in five minutes." Mrs. Redgrave replied.

Hines spotted Phil as soon as they drove into the park. "I'm staying in the car." Luke said not realizing how loud he was because he was wearing headphones. Laurie was the only adult by the play area, so the introduction was easy.

Laurie and Sherri talked for over an hour. Sherri did not realize that she had not connected with another adult in meaningful conversation in a very long time. She was enjoying this as much as Hines. "We are going to grab a bite after the park. You and Hines are free to join us?" Laurie stood and motioned for Phil to come over. "Five more minutes, then it will be time to go."

"Ok!" Phil said as he darted back toward the monkey bars.

"I would love to...I mean, we would love to have lunch with you all." Mrs. Redgrave blushed due to sounding too eager to have a newfound friend. Through their interactions they realized that they lived around the corner from each other. This allowed Phil to frequently play hockey in the driveway with Hines after school just like he used to do with his dad. Mrs. Redgrave noticed that it had been weeks since the school called her to inform her about something that Hines did at school that required her attention. She was convinced that his friendship with Phil was helping him cope with his dad being overseas in the military. Hines had not asked about his dad as much as he did before he began to hang out with Phil. To be sure, Mrs. Redgrave did a surprise visit to the school to see how Hines was doing. Not hearing anything should have been a relief, but not knowing how Hines was doing throughout the day became another source of anxiety for her.

"Hi. I am Sherri Redgrave…." Mrs. Redgrave said after a short beep sounded after she pressed the intercom button outside of the school's main office.

"Yes, we all know who you are." The receptionist interrupted her while buzzing her in. "His teacher should be on her way down. I am sure she is expecting you." The receptionist assumed Mrs. Redgrave had an appointment with Hines's teacher.

"Is something wrong? What happened?" Mrs. Redgrave slung her purse onto the counter, and then rested her forehead in the palm of her hand.

"Do you have an appointment to see Mrs. Davis about Hines today?" The receptionist said while placing her hand over the mouthpiece of the phone so that they could not hear the question she was asking.

"No, no. I was just coming up to check on him. No one is expecting me." Mrs. Redgrave placed both of her hands flat on the counters and steadied her breathing.

"Oh. Sorry. Let us see if Mrs. Davis is available to talk. I think this just happens to be her planning period." The receptionist mumbled words to the person on the phone before pressing the button to end the call. She then dialed a series of numbers and called Mr. Davis's classroom.

"She will be right up. You can have a seat over there." She nodded toward the plush blue chairs that lined the wall. Mrs. Redgrave clutched her purse as if she was giving it a bear hug and plopped down in one of the chairs.

"Good morning Mrs. Redgrave. How can I help you?" Mrs. Davis's voice was pleasant and welcoming. It seemed to calm Mrs. Redgrave even more. Mrs. Davis explained that Hines had been doing much better. She explained that there were several kids who now hung out with him at the playground and who also sat with him at lunch. Other than a few outbursts and rude moments, Mrs. Davis had not witnessed anything like the episodes in the past. Compared to swearing at teachers, turning over desk, and pushing kids, his behavior was mellow and at a level where they could manage without calling home. Mrs. Redgrave was pleased to hear a semi-decent report for once.

"After you explained the root of Hines' acting out, it has armed us to help him cope better with missing his dad." Mrs. Davis explained.

"I appreciate you all being a part of my support team." Mrs. Redgrave sat up in her seat and squared her shoulders and nodded her head to affirm her satisfaction in the report. She shook her hand and went home. Later that afternoon, when Hines arrived home, Mrs. Redgrave asked him about his day.

"Hi Honey. How was your day?" As the words left her mouth, she realized that she had not asked him about his day all school year long. It was nearing the end of the school year and she refrained from asking him out of fear of what she may find out.

"Good!" Hines replied as he threw his backpack to the floor and pulled open the refrigerator door.

"Go wash your hands, please." Mrs. Redgrave eyes glimmered and dimples deepened as she realized her little boy had his joy back.

Jeff Meets Phil (and Hines Redgrave)

Mrs. Redgrave and Ms. Parker arranged for Hines and Phil to attend the same summer camp. They hung out together most of the day along with a few other kids who were in their class from the previous school year. The summer camp divided the kids by age and grade and placed them in separate rooms accordingly. Parents would drop off and pick up their children at the room designated for their age, child's age group.

"Do I have to?" Jeff did not know what he would prefer to do, but going to camp at the community center did not appeal to him at all.

Super Pencil & The Revenge of the Talking Televisions

"What is it about this camp that is causing you so much stress?" Mr. Whitman quickly glanced in the rear view mirror while trying to keep his eyes on the road.

"I don't know." Jeff turned looked down at the action figures that littered the back seat of his dad's car. Staying home to engage in a daylong epic adventure just seemed like more fun. Mr. Whitman allowed long silence. It gave Jeff more time to think, but the longer the pause the more nervous Jeff became because any moment he knew his father would say...

"Still waiting!" Jeff's head jerked up and he caught eyes with his dad in the rear view mirror. It never failed; his dad's follow up to his initial question would always scare him half to death.

"Will I have friends there?" Jeff asked.

"You will be fine. You are a great kid who makes friends really easily. You can tell me about everyone you meet when I pick you up later."

Mr. Whitman followed the signs down the long hallway that led them to the check-in area for Jeff's grade. "Ok. Love you son. Have a great day." Jeff was scooping out the room to see if there were any familiar faces in the sea of kids. Mr. Whitman hugged Jeff and exited the classroom after grabbing the packet of information next to the sign in sheet. The camp counselor had already begun to create groups for the first activity of the day.

"Good Morning! What's your name?" the counselor stretched her arms toward Jeff to welcome him into the group. "You will be in

Group 5. Everyone introduce by telling your name, school, and the favorite thing you do." Jeff was good at remembering names. He made eye contact with each person as they talked about themselves. That helped him remember what they looked like when he was trying to remember their names later.

"My name is Phil. I go to the Wheatland's and I like to play hockey and read superhero comics." Jeff sat up in his seat. He was next and he liked reading superhero comics too. He could not wait to reveal that to Phil.

"I like superhero comics too! My name is…"

"Crash!!" The sound of the door hitting the wall startled everyone in the room. "Hines! Slow down. Ssshhhh! You are interrupting the class." Everyone turned toward the door to see a tall lady with sandy brown hair and fair skin painted with freckles gripping the shoulders of a kid who had the same facial features as the lady he was with.

"I'm sorry! Where do we sign in?" A few of the camp counselors scurried over to aid her. As she was signing in the entire room was quite and focused on all the commotion going on at the door. Just then, Hines recognized his friend Phil from across the room.

"Phil!" Hines shook loose from his mother and ran to Group 5 and slid a chain between Phil and Jeff. Jeff slid to his right to allow the kid more room at the table.

"Ok. Two more minutes on your introductions." The camp counselor announced. Jeff attempted to make eye contact with the other members of their group, but they were all engrossed in Hines and Phil's interaction. Jeff knew who Hines was, but had never had any interaction with him. He had heard stories about him at school, but this was his first close encounter with Hines. "I like comic books too." Jeff repeated several times trying to finish his introduction. The other kids in the group did not even notice that Jeff was attempting to finish his introduction. They were distracted by Hines.

"Ok. Times up! Everyone line up. We are going to the gym." Jeff did not get a chance to finish introducing himself to the group. A couple of the kids joined in with Hines and Phil and a few others appeared to have found something in common from their introductions. Initially, Jeff was disappointed for not having the opportunity to completely introduce himself to the group, but the thought of going to the gym overrode those feelings quite quickly. "Basketball!" Jeff thought as he rushed to the door. A girl beat him to the front of the line, so Jeff got behind her. He noticed that she was almost the same height with him. He only got a glimpse of her profile. He could only see her long dark hair draped down to the middle of her back.

Jeff rushed to the cage and sorted through most of the balls to find one that was just right. None of them bounced quite like the balls that he had at home. He finally settled on one and launched a shot toward the rim from out of bounds. "Splash! Oooooh! That was wet!" Jeff looked around with his left shooting hand still extended over his head. No one seemed to notice or care that he made the shot from out of bounds. Most found a spot on the bleachers and pulled out their phones. After a few three boys and a girl entered the court. After selecting a ball, they ran to the opposite side of the floor. Jeff watched from the other half of the court and approached slowly while dribbling.

"Y'all playin' Thirty-Two? Can I get in?"

"Naw. 2 on 2. Get another and we can play three's." the tallest boy replied.

Jeff scoped out the gym. That group was playing soccer, others were playing dodgeball, and then you had those sitting on the bleachers playing on their phones. Jeff reluctantly approached the kids who were in his group. He was more familiar with them, so that made him comfortable.

"We need one!" Jeff yelled as he walked closer. Not sure they understood what that meant, so he tried again. "One of you guys want to play a game of 3-on-3?" His question got Phil's attention.

"Yeah. I'll play." Phil replied as he got up and jogged toward Jeff. Hines was playing a game on his phone, so he did not realize that Phil had left the bench.

"Whoa! Check this out Phil I finally made it to the next level!" Hines turned and tilted the screen of his phone in the direction where Phil was sitting. He wheezed as his head jerked up and his eyes searched the gym for Phil. He finally found him as he caught a bounce pass from Jeff and made a lay up. Hines felt butterflies in his stomach as Jeff and Phil slapped hi-five after scoring a basket. Hines forgot about his game and was losing lives as he watched Phil and Jeff make basket after basket.

"Game time!" Jeff said as his other teammate made the game-winning shot. "Hey, what's your name?" Jeff asked.

"Alex." she replied as she slapped hands with Jeff and Phil.

"It's Phil, right?" Jeff asked.

"Yea. What's your name again?" Phil replied.

"It's Jeff. Hey, you said you like comic books. I too." Jeff continued.

"Thump!" Jeff jumped back and Phil stumbled as Hines slapped the ball out of his hand as he and Jeff were talking.

"Ha! Ha!" Hines laughed loudly as he attempted to dribble the ball, but it was obvious that he did not do it too often. Phil ran toward Hines to steal the ball back from Hines. Jeff stood in the middle of the court for a few minutes. Once he realized that Phil was not coming back over, he just began to practice his free throws.

Jeff began to settle in on the routine of camp. It was not as bad as he thought it would be. Each morning, Phil was typically one of the first kids to be dropped off. The time Jeff arrived varied, but Phil would already be engaged with other kids when he arrived. For several mornings, Phil watched Jeff play by himself and often wondered how someone could have so much fun all alone. Jeff would take books from his backpack to read and then he would play with action figures or whatever he got his hands on.

"He He He." Phil chuckled.

"What are you laughing about?" Hines turned around when he noticed that Phil was looking at him, but over his shoulder. Phil had been watching Jeff for most of the day. He was intrigued, so he decided to approach.

"I wonder what he's doing." Phil asked Hines. All of the other kids turned and looked in Jeff's direction.

"Why do you care about what he is doing?" Hines began to tell another story to engage his crew.

"Hines Redgrave! Your mom is here." Hines and Phil did their special handshake that included a series of slaps and gyrations. "See ya tomorrow Phil!" Hines said as he ran past Jeff, accidentally knocking Jeff's books on the floor. Hines noticed, but he did not stop to help Jeff pick them up.

"I got it." Phil rushed over to help Jeff pick up the books.

"Thank you sir." Jeff replied.

"I have been watching' you all week. What are you doing?" Phil asked

"Saving the world!" Jeff replied, turning his focus back to his action figures.

"Saving the world from what?" Phil asked.

"There is a supervillain named Dr. Whiteout. He is trying to erase the brains of all of the kids in the word. But I must stop him before he sucks the life out of them." Jeff said as he pointed to the story that he had just written. Phil really enjoyed reading books at home but never did so at summer camp. After reading a few frames of the comic book, Phil asked reluctantly, "Can I play?"

Jeff paused, surprised by Phil asking to join him. "Certainly!" Jeff replied as he intently reached into his backpack and pulled out a pencil, paper, and two action figures for Phil.

For the next couple weeks, in the morning before Hines arrived or in the late afternoon after Hines was picked up, Jeff and Phil would read, write, and act out scenes from the superhero stories they created. They usually had more time in the afternoon after Hines than in the morning. This became the highlight of their day.

The Encounter

One morning, Jeff and Phil arrived to summer camp at the same time. Mr. Whitman and Mr. Parker greeted and shook hands as they watched their boys run to the corner of the room, sit on the floor, and begin to dig into Jeff's backpack.

"Have a blessed day!" Mr. Whitman said as he exited the room.

"Thank you so much." Mr. Parker replied with a smile that seemed to remain on his face for the rest of the morning.

Jeff and Phil played by the window. Phil could see Hines and his mother walking up the sidewalk. When Hines entered the classroom, he came over and engaged with Phil, not even acknowledging Jeff. This day, Phil noticed the sad look on Jeff's face, but continued to listen to Hines talk about how he was learning how to make his own video game. His brother was attending a class and he was learning from him. Jeff continued to play for a few minutes, then he gathered his action figures and moved to a nearby table.

"Hi Jeff!" Maria said as she walked into the room.

"Good Morning." Jeff replied before realizing whom he was speaking to. He turned and realized it was Maria.

"Wanna play Connect Four with me?" Maria asked as she sat at the table, already opening the box and removing the pieces.

"Sure!" Jeff's competitive nature kicked in. He threw his action figures into his backpack and helped Maria sort the pieces.

Later that afternoon, during lunch, Jeff walked over and sat next to Phil.

"Wanna trade?" Jeff pointed at Phil'schocolate chip cookies as he placed snacks on the table in front of Phil. Phil looked at the spread of snacks that Jeff had in front of him trying to see what would be a fair trade. "Goldfish!" Phil decided.

"Ooh. Cookies! Can I have some?" Hines walked up to the table, reached over and grabbed Phil's cookies and took a bit out of one.

"Hines! I was gonna trade those with Jeff." Phil said sheepishly as he reached for the plastic sandwich bag, but stopped short of making contact with Hines' hand.

"Who?" Hines looked around Phil and made eye contact with Jeff. "Oh. Him? Too Late! Ha! Ha! Ha!" Hines laughed as he stuffed the entire cookie in his mouth.

"Sorry Jeff." Phil dropped his head and rolled his eyes. Jeff was upset. Not only did Hines take the cookies that he was about to trade for, but also now Phil did not have a snack to eat with his lunch. Jeff's mom always taught him to share. Jeff poured some of this Goldfish onto Phil's napkin and walked away from the table. Avoiding conflict was a lesson his dad often talked about. "The best fight is the one you never get into. Just walk away." Jeff heard his dad's voice in his head as he glanced back over his shoulder. Jeff had memorized the statement, but did not quite understand what it meant until now. Phil could sense that this ordeal made Jeff feel bad. He did not like the way Hines treated Jeff and this was not the first time Hines intervened while he and Jeff were talking. Phil was a little intimidated by Hines, so he never said anything to Hines about his rude behavior toward Jeff.

One stormy afternoon, all of the parents were late due to the storm. The thunder and lightning made Hines anxious, so he asked the camp counselor if he could go to the restroom. Hines did not want anyone to see that he was nervous because of the thunder and lightning. The bathroom did not have windows which provided Hines an opportunity to calm down for a little while until his mom arrived. As Hines exited the classroom, Jeff and Phil thought Hines was leaving for the day, so they continued with their normal routine of reading, writing, and pretending to save the world from evil villains. When Hines returned from the bathroom, he saw Jeff and Phil engaged in an epic battle. The colors of Hines' eyes seemed to change to match his skin-tone. Hines' brow was wrinkled as he clenched both of his fists tightly. He charged toward Jeff and Phil and kicked Jeff's backpack.

"What are you doing playing with this loser?" Hines said to Phil, interrupting their epic saga.

"I am not a loser!" Jeff countered. His reflexes did not give him time to think about what his dad taught him.

Gasps filled the air from the other kids because no one had ever stood up to Hines before.

Hines's voice got deeper. "If I say you are a loser, then you are a loser! The bigger boy snarled menacingly as he swiftly took steps in Jeff's direction.

Hines quickly peeked over to make sure that the camp counselor was not paying attention before he launched more verbal assaults at Jeff. "And look at the clothes you are wearing! Where did you get those clothes from? They look like my grandma's tablecloth!"

Laughs and giggles echoed through the room, but nothing out of the ordinary to get the attention of the camp counselor. More kids were gathering around. Many of them were pointing and laughing at Jeff due to the things that Hines was saying about him. Jeff was feeling pretty embarrassed, so he backed down. Tears began to form in Jeff's eyes because he was so upset. Jeff turned to walk away, to avoid the confrontation, but the taunts continued.

"Look! The li'l baby is about to cry!" Hines whimpered in a toddler's voice. "Let's go, Phil, you don't want to be seen hanging with crybabies." Hines wrapped his arm around Phil's shoulder and started to lead him away.

"Crybaby, crybaby!" Taunts came from other kids as they piled on Hines's teasing.

"*Enough!*" Phil said angrily as he shook Hines's arm off his shoulder and moved away from Hines. Jeff stopped and turned his head back toward the crowd.

Hines was surprised and fired back, "What? You heard me, Phil! I said, let's go! Now!" Hines took two brisk strides toward Phil.

Jeff turned quickly, matching Hines's strides, and stood side by side with Phil. "He said *enough*!" Jeff exclaimed with a bravado that even surprised him. Hines paused, secretly intimidated by Jeff's and Phil's united stance against him.

"What's going on over there?" asked the camp counselor. The crowd of kids quickly dispersed as if nothing was happening.

Hines burned with envy inside. He had just been embarrassed in front of the other kids, and his best friend had sided with Jeff. As Hines walked away, he bumped shoulders with Jeff and whispered in a growling voice, "This is not over, Jeff. You just wait! I will get revenge!"

Friends till the End

"Thank you for standing up for me, Phil." Jeff's expression was full of gratitude.

"No problem. That's what friends are for," Phil replied.

"Sorry about all of this. I know that Hines is your friend," Jeff said.

"Yeah, well, I thought he was, but real friends don't treat friends that way."

Jeff and Phil became even closer for the rest of summer camp, they continued to enjoy writing and reading superhero comic books and then pretending to save the world. After the incident with Hines, Phil and Jeff began to play throughout the day instead of just at the start and end of the day. They were already engaged when Hines arrived at camp. Hines was not happy to see them playing, but as he did not have the courage to confront both of them,

Hines regretted being mean to Phil, but did not know how to tell him. One afternoon, Hines saw Jeff leave classroom. "Here is my chance." Hines thought as he approached Phil.

"What's up Phil." Hines said.

"Hey Hines." Phil replied.

"Wanna come over later to play hockey?" Hines asked.

Phil took a moment to think about his answer. "I will have to ask my mom."

"Ok. I will have my mom call your mom." Hines said as he noticed Jeff entering the classroom. He thought Jeff was gone for the day.

"Ok, see ya." Phil said as he picked up Jeff's backpack and walked to the other side of the room. Jeff hesitated and did not approach when he saw Phil talking to Hine. "I don't want any trouble." Jeff thought as he watched from across the room.

Hines rejoined the circle with the other kids in his crew. He watched Jeff and Phil perform a series of slaps and gyrations similar to the cool handshake that he and Phil used to have. He felt as though Jeff had taken the only true friend he'd ever had. Hines vowed to seek revenge. He watched and plotted for his chance to even the score with Jeff.

Back to School—as Fifth Graders!

"Summer vacation always goes so fast!" Jeff said to Billy as they walked together on the first day of school. "This is our last year in elementary. I wonder what middle school will be like next year." Jeff and Billy were bummed to find out that they were not in the same fifth-grade class together. They figured they would still see each other at lunch and recess, though.

"Hey, there's Phil!" Jeff said to Billy. "Phil!" Jeff yelled out to Phil, who was walking with a group of kids ahead of them. "Phil is a really cool kid, you will really like him. He is the one with the blond hair carrying the skateboard." Jeff said to Billy as he started to jog lightly. "Come on; I will introduce you." Jeff turned back to notice that Billy was still walking. Billy did not jog with Jeff, so he was far behind when Jeff caught up to Phil. "Phil, whose class are you in?" Jeff asked.

"None of your business, goofball!"

Jeff was so excited to see his buddy Phil that he did not notice whom Phil was walking next to: Hines Redgrave.

Jeff looked Hines straight in the eyes for a few seconds. "Whatever to you, Redgrave!" Jeff dismissed Hines and continued to talk to Phil.

Hines looked at Jeff's clothes to figure out an insult to say, but they were actually nice, so he moved on to something else. "Look at your hair! It looks like you have little worms living on top of your head. Ha! Ha!" Hines said as he jumped off of his skateboard and carried it over his shoulder.

The couple of the other kids smirked as Hines continued his insults. "And why you always got that ball, you still ain't gon be good enough to make the team next year!" Jeff glanced over at Hines, shook his head from left to right and continued catching up with Phil.

After the incident at summer camp a couple years ago, Jeff asked his dad about how to handle bullies if he ever encountered them. Mr. Whitman was curious why Jeff would bring it up, so he asked him if he was being bullied. Jeff thought that it would make matters worse by involving his parents so he did not tell his parents about the summer camp incident. Jeff had many conversations with his dad about how to handle bullies and even role-played with him to practice bully situations. Mr. Whitman was not certain if Jeff was being bullied and not telling him, so he wanted to be sure that he was prepared. Mr. Whitman also frequently affirmed Jeff to ensure he was confident about who he is and that he did not have to believe the mean things that bullies said about him. Well, it worked. Hines no longer intimidated Jeff. Throughout fourth grade, Hines still fed off of Jeff's fear and insecurities. Jeff continued to avoid conflict with Hines by walking away. Now in fifth grade, Jeff had grown a few inches and gained a few pounds and was more self-assured about who he was. This confidence enabled Jeff to shake off the verbal attacks more quickly.

Hines did not know how to handle Jeff's newfound bravery. It actually irritated Hines that Jeff was so unfazed by all of his put-downs. Eventually Hines backed down when he realized that Jeff was not reacting to his name-calling. Phil noticed the grimacing look on Hines' face. It angered Hines that Phil was still talking to Jeff.

Phil had hesitated to answer Jeff's question in front of Hines, so Jeff asked him again. "Phil, whose class are you in?"

"Mr. Firestone's," Phil finally answered.

"Mr. Firestone's? Me too!" Jeff was excited to find out that he and Phil were *finally* in the same class. Hines gasped with frustration when he overheard Jeff and Phil were in the same class. He slammed his skateboard on the ground and forcefully pushed through the crowd. It really burned Hines, because he was in Mrs. Lebanski's class and not in Mr. Firestone's with Phil. As Hines approached the intersection, the crossing guard heard the sound of the skateboard wheels on the pavement and turned just in time to grab Hines' arm before he rolled into the middle of the street. "Hey! What are doing! Trying to get yourself killed? Slow down and wait until I say it's time to cross." Luckily, the cars at the intersection noticed Hines approaching on the skateboard.

In the several years since the incident at summer camp, Phil and Hines remained connected. Phil had never told his mother about what happened; therefore, their parents continued to plan times for them to hang out. Phil would make excuses about why he did not want to hang out with Hines, so they did not hang out as much as they used to. Phil would ask his mom if he could go to Jeff's house instead, but because Hines and Phil lived so close to each another, it was easier for their parents to get the two of them together. Phil was also afraid of what Hines might do if he found out that he did not want to hang out with him anymore, so sometimes, Phil just conceded.

Jeff turned and noticed that Billy was still walking far behind him. Jeff waved his hand, motioning Billy to hurry and catch up. Billy finally caught up to the crowd as the crossing guard stopped the kids to allow the cars to pass.

Super Pencil & The Revenge of the Talking Televisions

"Phil, I want you to meet my friend Billy. He is new to the neighborhood and lives on my street."

Billy and Phil made an awkward-looking gesture, kinda like a wave, to acknowledge each other.

"Billy's got Mrs. Lebanski, though. We can still hang out at lunch and recess," Jeff explained. "Oh, and that's Redgrave." Jeff pointed in Hines' direction.

Hines was surprised that Jeff had just introduced him to Billy. Hines and Billy quickly made eye contact and then turned away. Hines fought back a smile because being acknowledged by Jeff actually made him feel special, but he did not want Jeff to notice. "Wait a minute. Jeff said that his friend Billy was in *my* class." That realization turned his smile back into evil smirk. Hines's thoughts shifted as he replayed Jeff's introduction, remembering that Billy was in the same class as him. "What's your name again?" Hines nudged Billy on his right shoulder.

"Who me?" Billy did a double take, not wishing to make eye contact with Hines. "Oh. Uh. Billy."

"I've never seen you before. You new here?" Hines asked. Hines began to plot how he could come between Jeff and his new friend Billy.

Chapter 4

Hines's Plotting Begins

Jeff and Phil really enjoyed being in the same class. This gave them the opportunity to talk so much more. The students' desks were arranged in groups of four. Their desks were situated so that each set of four students faced one another. Mr. Firestone called each group of four a *pod*. Jeff and Phil were not in the same pod, but their pods were side by side so that Jeff and Phil sat with their backs to each other. Without turning, they could pass their latest comic-book creations by putting their arms down at their sides and then reaching behind them. Throughout the day they would pass comic-book ideas without being noticed by Mr. Firestone.

Well, sometimes! One time they got caught because they were too excited.

Phil had let out a gasp after reading the title of the comic Jeff had passed him. "*Super Pencil!*" Phil said aloud, before catching himself.

"Ssshhh!" Jeff did not want anyone to know about his latest masterpiece. Phil continued to chuckle at the title.

"I'm not done yet. My dad and I are working on this one together," Jeff explained. Mrs. Firestone walked toward them, so Jeff and Phil straightened up in their seats to appear as though they were paying attention.

"I'll take that." Mr. Firestone extended his hand toward Phil, then Jeff. He did not know which one had what they were passing. "I saw you pass a paper. So, let's have it. We can read it to the entire class."

"Please no!" Jeff did not want the entire class to know what he was writing about, especially if they were going to respond like Phil did.

Mr. Firestone sensed Jeff's desperation, so he just took it and decided not to read it before the class. Mr. Firestone surveyed the pages and then looked at Jeff. "We will talk about this later." Mr. Firestone walked to his desk and placed the pages in the top left drawer of his desks and continued to address the class. Later that afternoon, Jeff waited for all of the students to leave the class. He stopped by Mr. Firestone's desk.

"Can I please have my comic book back?" Jeff asked.

"Yes you can, Jeff. Actually, I wanted to tell you that this is really good storyline. I read it over my lunch period. Keep working on it, but just not during my class."

"Yes sir." Jeff placed the papers in a folder and put it in his backpack. He slung the backpack over his shoulder and ran out the door. He did not miss walking home with Billy and crew. "See you tomorrow." Jeff yelled as he ran out the classroom. "Walk!" Mr. Firestone replied.

Jeff and Phil still only talked and played at school since they had to rely on their parents to connect them outside of class. But they only had to wait one more year. That was when their parents had promised they would be old enough to walk to each other's homes without parental supervision.

After school, Jeff and Billy continued to draw all of the kids in the neighborhood to participate in their epic sagas. However, during recess and lunchtime, Jeff mostly played basketball and other sports with the other kids. Jeff was always intentional about selecting Billy to be on his team, but Billy did not like to play sports with Jeff as much as he enjoyed reading comic books and pretending to save the world. After a few weeks, Billy decided not to play sports with Jeff and the other kids during recess. When Jeff called his name to be on his team, he shook his head to indicate that he did not want to play.

"Come on, B, you're on my team!" Jeff insisted.

Billy declined and walked away, and sat down on the bench adjacent to the basketball court.

"About time you stopped hanging with those dorks!" Hines said as he walked up behind Billy.

Billy did not recognize the voice, but the proximity of the voice startled him. His head snapped around to see who it was. When Billy realized it was Hines, he turned back around and continued to watch Jeff and the other kids play basketball. "That's Hines Redgrave. He is one of the popular kids. He could not be talking to me." Billy thought.

"Jeff is not that good of a player anyway—look at him." Hines giggled as he came around the bench and sat next to Billy. Hines continued to say silly things and make jokes about Jeff and the other kids.

"Look at his feet. They are as long as skis!" that eventually made Billy giggle a little. Billy sensed that something was going on between Hines and Jeff, but he did not recall Jeff ever saying anything bad about Hines.

Over the next several days and weeks, Hines continued to befriend Billy by talking to him in class and inviting him to sit with him and his crew during lunch. For the first time in many schools, Billy felt like he belonged when he was around Hines and his crew. Billy started to like being around them.

One afternoon, Jeff entered the cafeteria looking for Billy so that he could sit with him. However, Billy was already sitting with Hines and his crew. Billy turned to look over his shoulder and made eye contact with Jeff as he entered the cafeteria. Billy slid to his right, making a spot for Jeff to sit next to him. Jeff began to walk toward Billy as he surveyed the rest of the table. But then Jeff realized that Billy was sitting next to Redgrave and his crew! Billy had just made room for him to sit between him and Redgrave! "Wait a second. Billy is at the table with Redgrave and his goons. I will end up sitting right next to Redgrave. I mean, I ain't scared of him, but no need to start something, especially by sitting right next to him." Jeff thought as he walked toward the table. Hines's back was to Jeff, so he did not see him approaching. In that instant, a few of Jeff's classmates called his name and waved for him to sit with them. Jeff changed direction and sat with them. "Whew, that was close. Sorry Billy," Jeff thought to himself.

Billy turned to find out what was taking Jeff so long. He looked around the cafeteria and saw Jeff laughing a few tables away. "Wait. What? Why is he sitting over there? Did I do something to make him mad at me?" Billy thought. Billy started to get up to go over to make sure that Jeff was ok. "Have you completed that game Billy?" Another kid at the table asked Billy, which stopped him from getting up.

Later that afternoon, Jeff and Billy walked home together from school. This day was much different than normal. Typically, they would catch up on everything that happened throughout the day and discuss what epic battles they would fight after they finished their homework. However, today there was an awkward silence. Jeff was contemplating asking about Hines and Billy's interactions over the past few weeks.

"How could Billy like a kid like Redgrave? How could anyone like a kid like that?" Jeff thought. "Wait. I never told him about our past. I gotta warn Billy about Redgrave. I should have said something when I first saw him talking to B by the basketball courts. It's only a matter of time before Redgrave starts tripping on him too." Jeff continued to think about what to say. "Well, just because we don't get along does not mean that B and Redgrave can't hang out."

At the same time, Billy was wondering why Jeff did not come sit with him during lunch like he always did. "Did I do something wrong?" Billy thought. Just then, Jeff saw something flashing in Billy's backpack, and Billy realized Jeff could see the flashing lights. It was from a light-up invitation; Hines had made Billy promise not to tell Jeff about his party. Billy felt horrible about keeping a secret from Jeff. Jeff thought this was a good way to break the awkward silence, so he asked Billy about the flashing light. Billy hesitated, but could not handle the thought of keeping a secret from Jeff.

Jeff asked again, "What's that flashing light?"

Simultaneously Billy asked, "Are you going to Hines's Halloween party?"

They both laughed out loud because they'd blurted out at the same time.

"You first!" Billy said.

"No, you go!" Jeff insisted, so Billy asked again.

"What party?" Jeff replied. Billy pulled the black skull-shaped invitation out of his backpack. The eyes on the invite were blinking with red lights.

Jeff gasped. "That's spooky!"

"I know, right? It's cool!" Billy replied cheerfully.

"If you think spooky is cool, then…" Jeff shrugged his shoulders while tilting his head to the side. "I noticed that you and Redgrave have been hanging out lately." Jeff could not resist this moment to subtly warn Billy about Hines. "Be careful. Something tells me he is up to something."

"No, he's cool!" Billy rebutted as he jogged ahead.

"You coming back out after you finish your homework? Four thirty, right?"

"No, Hines is coming over to play video games. Maybe you can come play too?" Billy replied.

The thought of Redgrave being on his street gave him goosebumps. He waved at Billy as he punched in the code to the garage door. He appreciated the invite from Billy, but Jeff did not have any intentions of joining them.

The Stake Out

Hines knew Billy and Jeff lived very close to each other, but he did not know how close. Hines discovered that Jeff lived only a few houses away, he often came to Billy's house to play so that he could spy on Jeff from Billy's bedroom window. As Billy and Hines played video games, Hines sat on the large beanbag under Billy's window. From where he sat, Hines could see Jeff playing outside with several other kids.

"Hey, there's Jeff!" Billy said when he saw him from his bedroom window. Billy ran to the window, opened it, and yelled to get Jeff's attention. "Hey Jeff, wanna come over to…"

"What are you doing?" Hines yelled as he yanked Billy by his left leg, knocking him on the floor. Hines rolled on top of him, with his palms pressing against Billy's chest. "Don't invite that loser over to play video games with us!"

"But, why not?" Billy asked.

Hines thought quickly fabricated an excuse to justify why he tackled Billy. "I mean, someone told me he does not like playing video games with *you*."

Jeff looked up, thinking he'd heard someone calling his name. The voice sounded like Billy's, but when he looked toward Billy's house he did not see anyone in the window, so he continued to shoot the basketball. "Three, two, one! *Buzz!* And Jeff hits the game-winning shot for the championship!" Jeff whispered to himself. "And the crowd goes wild!"

Billy sat down and continued to play the video game as thoughts raced through his mind. "Is that why Jeff's been acting weird lately? He does not like hanging out with me?" Billy's eyes saddened and he dropped his head.

Hines noticed Billy's expression change after he told him that Jeff did not like playing video games with him. Hines knew he had planted his first seed of destruction between Jeff and Billy's friendship.

Hines peeked back out the window as Billy looked downward. Jeff was gone. Jeff had gone inside to ask his mom if Phil could come over.

"Actually, I just texted Mrs. Parker, and she will be dropping him off before she goes to the grocery store," Jeff's mom replied.

"Yes!" Jeff exclaimed. He skipped toward the refrigerator to get a bottle of water.

"Go wash your hands!" Jeff's dad yelled when he saw Jeff reaching for the refrigerator door.

After grabbing a bottle of water, Jeff went to the front door to watch for Phil. Just then, Mrs. Parker's car was stopping in front of the house. At Billy's house, the sound of the car door closing got Hines's attention. He turned and saw a familiar silver four-door car. "Is that Phil's car?" Hines speculated. Hines fumed when he saw Phil walking up to Jeff's driveway. Hines began to reminisce about when Phil used to come to his house to hang out. Phil had not come over since the school year had begun. Seeing Phil at Jeff's house confirmed his suspicions about Jeff and Phil hanging out more because they were in the same class. "He was my friend first!" Hines mumbled as his eyes turned red and if he had been in cartoon steam would have flowed from his ears.

"What'd you say, Redgrave?" Billy asked.

"Hey! *Do not* call me that! My name is Hines! You call me *Hines*!" Hines scolded Billy in a frustrated rage.

Billy backed down. "Geeeeezzze, OK! What has your undies all up in a knot? Er, Hines," Billy added in a whisper.

Jeff was the only one who called Hines by his last name. Hines despised anything that made him think about Jeff.

"I love playing video games much more than I like playing outside," Billy proclaimed.

Hines's facial expression began to shift from an angry snarl to a menacing smile. "That's it!" Hines thought. "All kids like video games!" Billy's statement gave him an idea about how he could get more of the kids in the neighborhood to play video games indoors with him instead of pretending to save the world outside in the sun, cool breezes, with Jeff. Actually, when Hines thought about it, he realized playing outside sounded pretty cool, but that was not the point. His objective was to make sure that Jeff had no friends in the whole wide world! "I got it! We can create our own video game!" Hines exclaimed.

"Our own video game? How will we do that?" Billy replied.

"My brother, Luke, is really good at this computer coding stuff, and he has been teaching me too. Anything that we do not know how to do, he can show us. He can teach you too!"

"Let's go!"

Hines jumped up, grabbed Billy by the hand, and ran down the stairs.

"Mom, I'm going to Hines's—" Billy said in a rush as the door slammed behind them. They jumped on their bikes and flew past all the other kids.

"What's up, Billy? Redgrave?" Jeff greeted.

Billy was so caught up in the moment that he did not respond. Jeff, Phil, and the others continued to play after briefly wondering why they were in such a hurry.

When they arrived at Hines's house, Billy and Hines ran upstairs to his room and slammed his bedroom door behind them. Hines plopped down at his desk and flipped open his laptop. "One day, all of those kids will be part of my crew, and none of them will want to be friends with Jeff," Hines Redgrave whispered under his breath.

Chapter 5

Jeff's Big "Date"

Jeff and Maria's paths had crossed many times since first grade. Jeff's first memory of Maria was from summer camp, before third grade. He remembered marveling her jet-black long hair that streamed down her back like a waterfall. The caramel tone of her skin was created contrast for how her hair framed her face. Jeff did not quite understand why it felt like butterflies filled his stomach every time he looked into her almond shaped brown eyes. He tried to avoid eye contact as much as he could. His eyes would move down to her smile, but looking at her perfectly shaped white teeth and the two dimples on her right cheek captivated him even more. So he tried to focus on her shoes so that she would not catch him staring at her. They were always properly color coordinated with her shirts. Maria was also one of the smartest girls in his fourth-grade class. She was always first to raise her hand and she never answered a question incorrectly. That inspired Jeff to focus on his homework so that he could answer questions during class as well. "Maybe she will notice me if I answered questions." Jeff thought. Little did he know, it worked. Jeff's corky commentary which he added to his answers always made Maria laugh, but because she sat three seats in front of Jeff, he could not see her smiling as he answered questions.

On the last day of fourth grade, Maria's friend Gracie informed Jeff that Maria "liked-liked" him.

"Hey Jeff, Maria said that she 'Like-like' you!" Gracie said as she jogged to catch up to him before he exited the school.

Jeff took a glance back and saw Gracie approaching and Maria standing further down the hallway. "What does 'like-like' mean?" Jeff thought to himself as he took a step into the sunlight of the afternoon.

"Jeff, wait. Are you going to give Maria a kiss before you leave for the summer?" Gracie asked Jeff. "That's what people who 'like-like' each other do."

Jeff stopped walking. Now standing in the sunlight, he could not see Maria walking toward him down the hallway. It appeared dark inside the school because the sun was so bright outside. As Maria got close enough to hear Jeff's response, he said, "No, I am not ready for that right now," Jeff smiled, waved, and walked away. When he turned away his eyes widened, heart bounded in his chest, and he began to breathe rapidly. "Why did I say no?' Jeff peeked back and saw Gracie talking to Maria next to the bike rack. He turned his head quickly when it appeared as though they were looking in his direction. "I think I wanted to kiss her, but my mom always told me if a girl asked me to do something like that to say I was not ready." Jeff continued to ponder why he responded without hesitation. Knowing what to say helped him handle the situation. Jeff could not wait to get home to tell his mom and dad what just happened.

Throughout the summer Jeff often thought about Maria. He was flattered that a girl wanted to kiss him. "Maybe in fifth grade, I will be ready." Jeff and Maria had been in the same class since second grade, so the thought of her not being in his class didn't cross his mind. Jeff and Phil were the first students to enter Mr. Firestone's classroom on the first day. Jeff found his seat and searched the nametags nearby to find Maria's name. He did not see her name on the desk around him. "I found it." Phil yelled assuming that Jeff was trying to help him find his seat. Mr. Firestone emerged from the classroom attached to theirs. "Good Morning! Uhh, Jeff and Phil?" Mr. Firestone greeted after scrolling down his seating chart. "Yes sir!" Jeff replied as he looked toward the door at a rush of kids entering the classroom. He was disappointed that he did not have a chance to inspect the rest of the desk, but he just watched the door anticipating Maria's arrival. After a few minutes, no additional students walked through the door. Jeff gazed around the room and all of the seats were filled. "What!" Jeff suddenly grasped the fact that Maria was not in his class. He blank-stared into space for a long period of time. "Whom am I supposed to admire after I broke my pencil on purpose just to walk to the sharpener? Whom am I supposed to compete with to answer all of the questions correctly?" Jeff was so stunned; he did not hear Mr. Firestone calling his name for attendance. "Jeff Whitman. Jeff. Jeff. Jeff Whitman!" "Oh! Yes Sir! Here!" Jeff replied and then laid his head on his desk as his heart sank into his stomach.

A similar scene played itself out in Mrs. Lebanski's classroom. Maria was one of the first to enter the class. She walked from desk to desk reading the nametags. "Maria L." she found her name, but quickly glanced at the nametags around her. None of them had the first letter of their last name on their nametag. "There must be another kid named Maria in the class." Maria whispered as she stood next to her desk. Not seeing Jeff for the entire summer, she eagerly watched around the door waiting for him to enter. She was distracted by all of the new students that entered the classroom. The stream of students slowed to a trickle. She surveyed the room and noticed empty desks four rows over parallel to hers. Just then, a new girl dropped her backpack on top of that desk. Maria plopped down in her seat looking down at her desk. "Is he ok? Did he go to a new school? Whom will I compete with to answer all of the teacher's questions?" Maria slightly panicked as all of these questions about Jeff flew through her mind.

Maria began to reminisce about the day she noticed Jeff. It was in third grade. Mrs. Davis was going over their geography study guide. She asked the class if anyone knew what the largest river in the world was. Maria was always the first to raise her hand to answer the question, but this time Jeff blurted out the answer. "It's the Amazon! It's four thousand three hundred and forty-five miles to be exact. Well, some say that the Nile is largest because its drainage basin covers eleven countries, but the Amazon has the most water. But, you might not want to swim there. They are known for having some of the largest crocodiles in the world!" Maria eyes cut to the side to see who answered the questions so swiftly. She was stunned. Not only did Jeff give the correct answer, but also he offered the same background that she was going to add to her exam next week.

"Maria. Maria Lopez." Mrs. Lebanski's low toned voice shook Maria from her daydream. She looked around as some of the kids snickered at her reaction. Their laughter reminded her of how students used to make fun of her when she was always the first and only one to answer the teacher's questions. "Teacher's pet. Teacher's pet." Would hum in the background every time she raised her hand or gave the correct answer. Well, that was until Jeff began to challenge her to be the first one to raise his hand. Maria went throughout the week and her and Jeff's path never seemed to cross.

"Hi, Maria. Oh no, what happened to your leg?" Jeff noticed that Maria was walking on crutches as she exited the car. It was Friday morning, and this was the first time Jeff had seen Maria all week long.

"I fell riding my Hoover Board and sprained my ankle pretty badly," Maria replied with a gasp when she turned to see that it was Jeff.

"Oh man, that sounds painful," Jeff said sympathetically.

After a few moments of talking, Maria asked Jeff, "Want to stay in during recess and play with me today?"

Jeff's heart began to race, and the palms of his hands were dripping with sweat when he realized what Maria had just asked him to do. He was not sure why a simple question would make him feel this way. Jeff was thrilled about the thought of eating lunch with Maria. He zoned out, daydreaming about all of the things he could do to embarrass himself while eating lunch with her. Jeff was unsure how to answer her question. After a few moments of Jeff staring off into space, Maria called his name a few times to get his attention. Maria's voice got a little louder each time. By the third time, it was loud enough to startle Jeff and get the attention of the other students walking past them. "Jeff!" Maria shouted.

Jeff was mortified once he realized what he had just done. His embarrassing antics had started already. "I need more time to prepare," Jeff thought to himself. "Come on, Jeff, think quickly."

"Oh...well...huh...I already told Phil that I would play basketball with him today, so I will stay in with you on Monday," Jeff answered.

"OK, that's a date!" Maria said with a smile.

"OK, let me help you with your backpack." Jeff opened the door and carried Maria's backpack into the school and to her classroom. Maria was extremely appreciative of Jeff's courtesy.

"Wait a minute—did she say *a date?*" Jeff thought as he walked away.

Jeff replayed his conversation with Maria in his mind for the remainder of the day. Jeff could not wait to get home to talk to his father. "A *date?*" Jeff said to himself as he tossed his backpack in the corner of the mudroom and ran up the stairs to find his dad in his office. His dad was on the phone, working. "How can he work at a time like this? The world is coming to an end!" Jeff thought. His dad waved and put up his right index finger to remind Jeff that he must patiently wait and not interrupt him while he was talking on the phone. Jeff pressed his back against the frame of the door to his dad's office and slid down until he gently came to rest on the floor in the doorway of his father's office. His dad continued to talk on the phone for *hours.* Well, maybe it was only a couple of minutes, but it felt like hours to Jeff. Finally, his dad pulled the white earpiece out of both ears and laid the long cord on his desk. Jeff sprung to his feet to greet his dad.

"Hi, son, tell me about your day!" Jeff's father said. This was a common question that was typically followed by five more questions, because Jeff always gave one-word answers to his dad's open-ended questions. But not today.

Jeff jumped right in. "Sooooo, Dad, I have a *date* on Monday and…"

"A date!" Jeff's dad interrupted with a slight chuckle. "Son, slow down. You are too young to date." He laughed again. "A date? You need to borrow my car too?" Jeff's dad joked, affectionately rubbing the top of Jeff's head as he walked past him, exiting his office.

Jeff followed behind his dad, still attempting to explain the conversation he had with Maria earlier in the day.

"Do you have any homework? Do it now, because we have a long weekend ahead of us," his dad continued. Jeff was disappointed that his dad was not listening and did not ask anything more about his "date." Jeff retreated to his bedroom, still feeling the pressure of what lunchtime on Monday would bring.

Jeff always enjoyed the weekends with his mom and dad. They would plan at least one fun thing for them to do together, and they allowed Jeff to pick one restaurant for them to go to. However, this weekend, the only thing Jeff thought about was his "big date."

After the weekend festivities, it was Sunday night, and Jeff had just finished taking a bath. He walked down the hall and past his father's office, where he noticed the light of his laptop illuminating his dad's face. Jeff thought, "Here is my last chance!"

"Dad?" Jeff ventured.

"Yes, son?"

"What are you supposed to say to a girl when you're on a date?"

"Wait a minute. He is still thinking about this *date*?" Jeff's dad thought. "This is more serious than I thought. Wait, he may feel like I dismissed him on Friday, but two days later he is still thinking about this 'date' on tomorrow. A date?" Jeff's dad continued to muse while shaking his head side to side at the thought of having this conversation sooner than expected. He was not expecting to have this conversation with Jeff until he was in high school. However, he recognized that if he did not have this conversation with Jeff right now, his son would go on this "date" unprepared and nervous, which could impact his self-esteem for years to come.

"So, son, tell me about your date," Jeff's dad said finally.

Jeff was delighted to tell him the entire story. They walked into Jeff's room and sat on the floor, with their backs resting against the side of the bed. Jeff went on. "Well, Maria hurt her leg so she could not go outside for recess. She asked me if I could stay in with her during recess to play and eat lunch together. I told her I would on Monday and she said, '*OK, that's a date.*'"

"Maria?" Jeff's dad tried to recall her. Jeff had mentioned her name several times over the past two years. If this is the same Maria, they were in the same second, third, and fourth-grade class together. Jeff's dad thought, "Although I figure that Maria possibly may have only been using an expression, Jeff's perception was that it was 'a date,' so let's make sure he is ready."

"Well, son, on a date, the key is to get to know the other person. Ask them questions about themselves, such as 'What are your favorite things? What type of music do you like? What are your favorite hobbies? Which TV shows do you enjoy watching? What toys do you enjoy the most?' Ask them why they like those things so much, and then most importantly, *listen*! Learn the things that both of you like, then talk about the things you have in common," Jeff's dad instructed.

"OK. Thanks, Dad," Jeff said as he wrapped his arms around his dad's neck super tight. Jeff's dad knew that this was a hug of appreciation, and it made him feel really good. He did not have these types of talks with his dad, so he looked forward to being able to give father-son advice on milestone matters such as this.

Jeff's anxiety had subsided because he now felt ready for his "big date." Jeff's dad was beaming with pride after their father-son moment. After all, Jeff was his first and only son. He envisioned giving relationship advice to his son one day, but not this soon. It felt good to know that his son trusted him enough to come to him for guidance. Jeff's dad went downstairs to tell his wife about the conversation he'd just had with Jeff. The thought of their son going on a "big date" was bittersweet.

"So, your son has a date on tomorrow." Mr. Whitman started.

"A date? What do you mean a date?

Yeah. Some little girl named Maria asked if he could come over her house after school to…"

"What! Jeff! Mrs. Whitman called out.

"Baby, Baby! Wait! I'm playin'." Mr. Whitman wrapped his arms around Mrs. Whitman to stop her from going up to Jeff's room. Mr. Whitman continued to laugh.

"Don't play like that. I was about to go call that little girl's mother."

"No for real. You remember Maria? She hurt her leg and asked Jeff to stay inside during lunch to talk with her. So calm down, it's innocent.

"Innocent? This is how it begins."

"My lil homie is growing up." Mr. Whitman embraced his wife a little tighter. This experience made them both smile. It also made them a little sad as they realized that Jeff was growing up way too fast.

The next day, Jeff kept his word and met Maria in the cafeteria during their lunch period. "I'll take that!" Jeff said as he walked up behind Maria in the lunch line and swiped the tray out of her hand. Maria was still on crutches, but she insisted on doing everything herself. Jeff was the only person she allowed to assist her. Maria had not seen Jeff all day, so she had not been sure if he had come to school or if he would even remember he was supposed to eat lunch inside with her today.

"Heeyyy Jeff!" Maria was a little startled when Jeff popped up from behind. Maria was happy to see Jeff. She was beginning to worry that she was going to have to eat alone. "I was not sure you were here today. Thanks for carrying my tray." Their eyes made contact and they both looked away quickly as they blushed.

"Are you getting anything else?" Jeff asked.

"An apple juice, please." Jeff grabbed two apple juices, one for Maria and one for himself. After swiping his ID badge, he took Maria's from around her neck and gave it to the Lunch Lady. Jeff placed her ID back around her neck. He picked up her lunch tray with his left hand and strained to pick up his own with the other. Jeff walked away before as Maria braced herself with both crutches. The Lunch Lady admired how attentive Jeff was being towards Maria. "Girl, you betta keep him!" the lunch lady said. Maria followed behind Jeff not fully comprehending what the lunch lady was referring to.

Jeff found a place for them to sit at a lunch table in the corner. The table was perpendicular to the wall of windows. Jeff and Maria sat next to each other and could see all of their friends playing outside. Jeff remembered his father's advice and asked Maria all of the questions at once without giving her a chance to reply. Jeff fought making eye contact, because he did not want those butterflies to attack him again. Maria appeared to remember all of his questions and jump right in as soon as Jeff paused.

"It might sound silly, but I like to play dress-up in my mom's clothes. I pretend to be a fashion model on covers of magazines. I use my big sister's self-stick to take pictures. She helps me edit them on the computer. What do you like to do?"

"I don't think that's crazy. I..." Jeff said in a low tone as he peered the side of Maria's face. Maria continued without giving Jeff time to reply.

"But what I really love to do is read mystery novels. I like to try to solve the mystery by putting all of the clues together. My mom says I should be a lawyer or something, but I don't know."

"I like to write stories..." Jeff tried to jump in again.

"My mom does not allow me to watch TV that much. She calls it the idiot box. So I mostly watch YouTube videos on my phone. Do you have a phone yet?" Jeff shook his head no. "Do you watch TV? Not that you are an idiot, not everyone who watches TV is an idiot, but..." Maria paused and turned to look at Jeff who was still listening to every word that came out of Maria's mouth. She smiled when she realized Jeff was still listening. "I see you still like playing basketball."

Jeff paused, realizing that Maria was now waiting for him to reply. "Yes, Yes. I like basketball. I like to read stories too. But I like writing my own stories."

Maria answered, and then countered with the similar questions for Jeff. They found out that they had many things in common. They both had a great time together and hated that the lunch period had to end.

"Only five more minutes you two." The Lunch Lady said as she wiped down the table behind them. They both turned and saw her walking away. They looked back at their trays and realized that they had not eaten much of anything. They both hurried to take a few bits when a voice snarled from over Jeff's right shoulder. "What are you doing in here? All of your loser friends are outside!" Jeff and Maria turned to see who was talking.

"Redgrave! Good afternoon, sir." Tension filled the air. The bell rang. Jeff began to gather the trash. "You need help getting to class?" Jeff asked Maria.

"Not from you! I will help Maria!" Hines interrupted.

Jeff did not want to make a scene in front of Maria, so he just allowed Hines to assist her. Maria did not want to make matters worse, so she also permitted Hines to help her.

"Byyyyyeee Jeffffff!" Maria sang with a smile as Jeff walked away.

"See ya, Maria." Jeff smiled back at her. Jeff made eye contact with Hines as he walked away. "Good afternoon sir." Jeff said.

Hines turned away from Jeff and scowled. It irritated Hines even more that he no longer seemed to get under Jeff's skin, no matter how many insults he launched at him. It bothered him too that Jeff was hanging out with Maria. Hines thought Maria was the prettiest girl in the world. He sometimes stared at her while sitting in Mrs. Lebanski's class. Now that Hines understood that Jeff and Maria were friends, he knew he had to act fast.

Chapter 6

The Revenge of the Talking Televisions

"Ready to go sledding?" Jeff's dad asked as he put on his snow pants.

"Almost, I can't find my other boot." Jeff ran upstairs to ask his mother where it might be. Jeff knew not to ask his dad because his mom was always making fun of them both for not being able to locate anything. For weeks now, Jeff and his friends had not been able to enjoy playing in the snow due to subzero temperatures. Being inside during the winter months gave Jeff time to catch up on his reading and writing epic sagas. Reading other comic books gave him new ideas about how he could "save the world." He could not wait to unveil his new stories to his friends.

Hines was busy during his time indoors too. For months, he and Billy had been working on his new video game every day after school and on the weekends too. The storyline of the game portrayed a Big Bad Boss named Jeff who programmed all electronic devices with screens to brainwash the world's citizens and get them to follow him as their leader. The screens looked like robots with huge screens for heads. Because the robots basically looked like televisions with arms and legs, they were called "talking televisions."

The game was a multiplayer, team-based system that allowed people to play together while connected to Wi-Fi or through cellular data service. The object of the game was to destroy as many talking televisions as possible to prevent them from brainwashing the entire world. The talking televisions would latch on to the player with a head harness that would begin to suck the life out of them. The players received points for every talking television they destroyed and received bonuses for destroying a talking television that was connected to a teammate. When new players logged in to start a game, they could be invited to join an existing saga or start a new saga with their own group of friends. The game also allowed players to talk to one another by voice chat while playing the game and even share lives and weapons as they fought to defeat the evil villain. There were many levels to clear before the players could square off against Jeff, the Big Bad Boss. Though the players would encounter Jeff at every level, they never actually had a chance to fight him. At the end of each level, the Big Bad Boss retreated to plot another plan to take over the world, and then the players would proceed to the next level.

If the "talking televisions" got close enough to touch a player, the "talking television" would connect to the player, immobilizing that player until a teammate cut the cord or completely destroyed the "talking television" that was attached. The longer a player was attached to a screen head, the longer it would take for him to regain his energy and ability to help his teammates fight against the other talking televisions. Eventually, if a player was attached for too long, he would die. The object of the game was to destroy as many talking televisions as possible before all of your teammates were tethered or completely destroyed.

"Hey Luke, come check out my new game! Hines called for his brother from his bedroom. When Luke entered his room he watched Hines play the game.

"Impressive Lil Bro. You learn fast. Pretty soon the student may be better than his teacher." A rare smile wrapped Hines' face as his brother exited the room. Positive affirmation made him feel good, so he called for his mother to come see his game as well.

"Hey Mom! Come here. Look." Hines continued to destroy talking televisions as he waited for his mother. "Mom!" Hines yelled again after glancing back, not seeing his mother. So, he completed the level he was on, paused the game and walked downstairs to the family room. His mother was sitting on the couch talking on the phone.

"Mom!"

"I am on the phone buddy, just wait a minute. So like I said..."

Hines plopped down on the couch next to his mother. He wanted her to be proud of what he created, so he waited for her to get off the phone. His mother had been watching the nightly news before taking her phone call. During the program, the news anchor was reporting on the power of advertising.

"The purpose of advertising is to persuade people to do what you want them to do. It's sort of embedding subliminal messages to make them think, feel or act how you want them to."

"That would be great if I could get people to think and act how I wanted them to. I would make my mom get off the phone." Hines mumbled while giving his mother the side eye.

The news anchor continued, "Movie producers do it all of the time. They hide messages in the background of movies or write scripts to get people to think what they want."

"Yeah, sometimes people don't remember what is real and what is apart of the movie." the second news anchor joked.

Hines sat up in his seat. "Hidden messages? If it's possible to add hidden messages in movies, I wonder if you can add them to video games." Hines jumped up and ran back up to his room and sat at his desk. He began to search the Internet for how to program hidden messages in video games. He had a lot to learn. Well, for now, his game was fun to play. Hines was eager to get it in the hands of his classmates.

Hines asked his brother to show him how to share his game with his friends. After Luke texted Hines the steps and promised to help him get it loaded to the app store as well. Hines sent a text message with the link and access code for the game to Billy immediately. Hines figured if Billy liked it, so would all of the other kids who enjoyed "saving the world" with Jeff. Billy downloaded the app as soon as he received it. The game was so engaging; Billy was up all night playing it. He turned the backlight down on his phone and pulled the covers over his head so that his mother would not see the illumination of the screen.

"Hey Billy! Wait up." Hines jogged to catch up with Billy who was walking to school with Jeff Monday morning. Hines was so excited to learn what Billy thought of his game that he did not even acknowledge Jeff with his typical dig. "What did you think?" Hines looked over at Jeff realizing that he may have heard his question. So he grabbed Billy by the arm and stopped walking.

"What does he think about what?" Jeff thought, but he kept walking.

"It was cool. I kept dying. I could not figure out how to disconnect from the TV guy? There were too many to fight by myself."

"Yeah. Remember, the game is made for multiple players. You need someone else to kill them to set you free. But what did you think?" Hines started walking after he saw that Jeff was about ten yards ahead.

"I guess it was pretty cool. I stayed up late playing it, because I did not want to lose." Billy rubbed his eye to clean the crud from the corners.

"So do you think others will like it?" Hines asked

"Definitely. It was fun!"

About a week had gone by. Hines asked his brother almost daily if his app had been approved by the app store yet. Then, Saturday morning, Hines was awakened by the ding of his cell phone. He grabbed his phone and could make out that it was a text from his brother, but he could not read the entire text. He wiped his eyes and then reached for his glasses that were resting on the nightstand. "Your App has been approved!" Hines launched himself from the bed, drew open his blinds and raised his hands above his head with a loud shout of victory. "Yeeeesssss!" Hines spent the blustery winter weekend indoors texting and direct messaging all of his classmates with the free link and password to download his new video game on their laptops, tablets, or phones. "We will see how many friends you have now, Jeff Whitman!" Hines thought bitterly. Phil had been Hines's best friend since preschool, and Hines was resolute that he would not only win him back but also make sure that Jeff did not have any friends at all!

Hines's brother did not realize how much his little brother had actually learned by watching over his shoulder. He downloaded the game and began playing it. To his surprise, Hines had added additional features and details above and beyond what they had worked on together.

"Dude. This game is actually pretty cool." Luke said as he walked into Hines' room with his phone in hand.

"Thanks Luke."

On the surface, the Revenge of the Talking Televisions looked fun and innocent. However, after Billy went home and Hines's brother fell asleep, Hines added more features to enhance his diabolical plot against Jeff. Because of the nightly news story, Hines continued to research ways to add hidden messages into his game. He learned ways to encode hidden messages, such as "Jeff is the enemy" in the background graphics and to flash on the screen for milliseconds. Even though he was talking about the Big Bad Boss, his hope was for his classmates to associate the hidden messages with Whitman. "Play one more game," "You are almost there," "Playing indoors rules!" Hines wanted his classmates to have a stronger urge to play the video game indoors rather than pretending to save the world with Jeff outside. "Don't tell Jeff," "Hines is cool," and "Jeff sucks;" were other hidden messages that Hines inserted to flash on the screen. From Hines' perspective, these did not need an explanation.

Naming the Big Bad Boss "Jeff" was no coincidence. "Don't tell Jeff" was Hines's favorite subliminal message in the game. Hines did not send Jeff the link to the video game, and the message was Hines's way of ensuring that no one shared the video-game link with Jeff. Showing just how much Hines despised Jeff, every time players needed a friend to rescue them or share a new life, they had to scream "Jeff sucks" into their headsets. When they did, an indicator would appear on all their teammates' screens to go save their teammate from the talking televisions, or the indicator would prompt them to share a life so that their teammate could continue playing. "In my video game, we get to save the world, but I made it so I could destroy *your* world, Jeff Whitman!" Hines thought as he checked the number of downloads before going to bed.

Within a couple of days, nearly half of the students at school had the link to the game, and it had already become extremely popular. Many of the kids would secretly play the Revenge of the Talking Televisions on their phones during lunch or recess and on the computers in the learning resource center when they were supposed to be doing classwork. "Jeff sucks!" "Jeff sucks!" echoed around the lunchroom.

Jeff overheard Phil say, "Jeff sucks!"

"What did I do to you?" Jeff asked.

"Not you, silly!" Phil replied, looking up from his screen. "Jeff, the Big Bad Boss man! You don't have the new video game, the Revenge of the Talking Televisions? It's pretty cool!"

"What game? I don't know what you're talkin' about."

"Blah, blah, blah" is what Jeff sounded like to Phil. He was too distracted by his game to hear what Jeff was asking. At that moment, Phil received an instant message through the game from a kid on the other side of the lunchroom: "Don't tell Jeff!" Phil giggled and kept playing.

It was too cold to go outside, so the kids had indoor recess in the gym during lunch. Jeff was the first student to grab a basketball. He turned to throw the ball to Phil, but Phil was not behind him as usual. Phil and the other boys who normally sat with him were walking toward the bleachers with their phones in hand. Jeff walked over to Phil to ask if he wanted to shoot hoops. "Not today..." Phil said nonchalantly without even looking up at Jeff. "That was cold?" Jeff thought Phil's response was odd, because they always loved indoor recess. This gave him the chance to shoot on the glass backboard and to pretend to play for the gold medal in the Olympics. So, Jeff turned and walked and launched a shot toward the rim while standing from out of bounds. Swish! "Oh, Phil! Did you see that?" Jeff turned back to Phil, but because he had his ear buds in both ears, he did not notice Jeff had made the shot.

As he dribbled the ball, he glanced around the gym. All of the kids he typically played with had white cords dangling from their ears, with their eyes fixed on their screens. They were standing near the wall or sitting on the bleachers. "That's odd. That game could not be that good." He tried to distract himself by taking another shot. Whispers of "Jeff sucks!" echoed around the gym. "Jeff, it's only a stupid video game!" Jeff told himself. "Phil even said that they are not talking about you. Who would name a character in a game Jeff?" Jeff thought. Jeff did not understand how things could change so quickly. "Just a week or so ago, all of the kids were running around and shooting baskets. Now, they are all over there like zombies!" He felt like he was in a different world, but he just internalized his stress and pretended that he was not bothered by it all. "Three, two, one—at the buzzer!" Jeff whispered as he shot the basketball.

"Nice Shot!" Jeff had not noticed Maria walking into the gym.

"Thanks!" Jeff replied as he turned to see who complimented him.

"So, you not playin' that video game?" Maria asked

"Naw. I much rather do this." Jeff took another shot, but it bounced off the rim.

"What's the big deal with the game any ways?" Maria asked.

"I don't know. I have never played it." Jeff avoided eye contact and took a shot from the free throw line.

"Can I shoot?"

Jeff hesitated then walked the ball over to Maria instead of throwing it to her. "Sure." Jeff said as he handed her the ball.

Maria snatched the ball from Jeff's hands. "You could have thrown it, ya know. Girls can catch too." Maria smirked and walked to the free thrown line and took a shot. Swish!

"Good Shot!"

"Don't sound so surprised. I bet I can make more than you."

Super Pencil & The Revenge of the Talking Televisions

"Let's go!" Jeff smiled and accepted the challenge. "One for One. Two for two. Two for three." Jeff counted as Maria shot the ball. "Seven for ten. Pretty good. Do you play for the team?"

"No. I just shoot in my drive way with my brothers sometimes."

Before Jeff had a chance to shot, the bell rang. Lunch period was over. "Next time I will beat you." Jeff said. "Byyyyeeee Jeeeeffff" Maria sang as she exited the gym. Hanging out with Maria took Jeff's mind off the game. As Jeff walked to class, he looked for Phil, but he was talking and laughing with the other kids from his class. Jeff was walking behind them and could hear that they were talking about how they had almost "saved the world" in the video game. Jeff sped up to join the group, but when they noticed him, they all stopped looked at one another, giggled, and the conversation stopped. As they reached their classroom, Phil and Jeff turned to go into the class. A few of the other kids continued down the hall, but turned back and said, "Hey Phil. Don't tell Jeff." They all laughed out loud. "Don't tell Jeff what?" Jeff asked Phil. "Bro, they are talking about the game. Not you." Phil replied. Later that afternoon as Jeff was walking home from school. It was more of the same. Although Jeff was walking within the same crowd of friends, they had earbuds in their ears playing the video game as they walked down the sidewalk. Jeff and Billy turned to go down their street as the crowd kept straight. There were a few kids still walking with them. "Here comes Jeff." Billy said. Jeff thought Billy was talking to him, so he responded. "Hey, Billy. I have a new cool saga I started to write. It's called Super…" Jeff realized that Billy was not talking to him, but talking about the Jeff in the video game. Jeff could hear the sound effects of the game blaring from their ear buds. Jeff's head lowered and he watched the cracks on the sidewalk until he reached his house. Jeff did not know it was possible to feel alone when around so many people.

***

"Hey, Jeff! How was your day?" his dad asked as he came into the house from school.

"It was"—Jeff paused a little too long. "It was OK."

Jeff's dad sensed that everything was not actually OK. "So, tell me about your day?" Jeff's dad probed.

Jeff blurted everything out in a rush. "It'sonlyastupidgame, buteveryoneisplayingit! Theysaytheyarenotreallytalkingaboutme—who cares!"

"Jeff! Wait. Slow down. What game? Come sit down. Let's talk," Jeff's dad said calmly.

Jeff began to tell his father about what happened at lunch, but he did not have a full understanding of the video game, where it came from, or what it was about.

"Oh Jeff, it's just a coincidence. 'Jeff' is a common name. Afterall, you said it yourself, 'It's only a game.' I understand how it could make you feel to hear people say bad things about you—well, someone with the same name as you. But it is not you they are talking about. You said that they are not being mean to you, right?" Jeff's dad paused for a couple of seconds. "Besides, you know who you are. I understand that words can be very hurtful, but they can only hurt you if you believe the false things that people say. You are awesome! And don't let anyone tell you otherwise!"

Jeff's dad comforted him. Jeff liked talking to his dad. His dad always had the right words to make him feel better. "Thanks, Dad!" Jeff replied.

However, Jeff knew that something was still fishy about that video game. All of his classmates were playing it, and he did not know where it had come from. "I will get to the bottom of this!" Jeff thought as he hugged his dad, then he went to his room.

After about an hour, Jeff's dad strolled down the hall to check on him. He found Jeff in his room lying on a large blue area rug in the middle of the floor. It was plush and provided Jeff with a landing pad to do homework, write comic books, or play with his action figures. Jeff was lying on his stomach writing in the journal that his mom bought him. His dad could see doodles of action figures above the paragraph Jeff was writing.

"So, what is this great saga about?" Jeff's dad asked.

The question startled Jeff because he did not realize his dad was standing there. "Whew! You scared me." Jeff sat up and showed his dad his journal.. "It's called *Super Pencil*!" Jeff answered.

"That's an interesting title. Tell me more." Jeff's dad sat next to Jeff on his plushy blue area rug. Jeff's passion came alive when he began talking about this story. "It's about a world where the people are writing utensils instead of humans. Some kids are crayons; big kids are like--markers, and adults are pens, colorful pencils and paintbrushes. It is a colorful and creative world, because everyone leaves their own special mark wherever they go. But there is a villain named Dr. Whiteout. He is an evil scientist who wants to remove all of the color and fun from the world. He creates these robots that erase the color from everything that the kids make. Then if robots catch the kids, they begin to lose their colors. Once all of their colors are gone, they can never make creative things again. But this is a job for Super Pencil!" Jeff jumped to his feet pushed out his chest, while placing his hands on his hips. Jeff continued to describe Super Pencil and how he got his superpowers as he rustled through clothes on the floor of his closet. His dad did not know what he was looking for until Jeff emerged with his cape strapped on to his back. "Super Pencil fights against the evil plans of Dr. Whiteout to steal the color from all of the kids in the world."

Jeff's dad noticed a difference in the way he talked about this story, more passionately than any others. He assumed that it might have something to do with the conversation he had with Jeff a little earlier, so he wanted to Jeff sort through how he was feeling. "How about we write this one together?"

Jeff paused, not sure how to take his dad's gesture. "Sure. I think?"

Jeff's dad continued to explain how they could work together. "You imagine and I will write. We can develop the characters, the plot, and maybe this can be an epic saga that could be sold in the comic-book store we go to all of the time."

The thought of his comic book being sold in stores so everyone could read it got Jeff's attention. "Maybe even becoming a movie!" Jeff said as he began to catch the vision. "I can be the star actor—the superhero!" Jeff exclaimed as he jumped to his feet, placing his hands on his hips.

"Jeff, to me, you are already a superhero!" Jeff's dad beamed with pride.

"Thanks, Dad!" Jeff hugged his dad and began to write more in his journal.

Chapter 7
Summer Time Is Coming

There were only a couple more days left until summer vacation. Jeff had spent the last several weeks writing *Super Pencil* with his dad and doing sleuth work about the origin of the Revenge of the Talking Televisions.

"I am smart, I am cool, I am compassionate, I am a good athlete, and I write great stories…" Jeff repeated as he waited at the end of his driveway for Billy. Most morning, Mr. Whitman would go into Jeff's room to watch and pray over Jeff and Billy as they walked down the street. After about five minutes, Mr. Whitman opened the window. "Jeff, you should probably just start walking. Billy may not be going to school today." "Ok. Love you dad." Jeff replied as he started to walk. He continued to whisper positive affirmations as he walked by himself this day. "It does not matter what other people think of me: it matters most what I think of myself!" Jeff proclaimed. This repeated itself for the next couple days. Mr. Whitman made a note to ask Jeff if Billy was in school or to text Mr. Ramirez to make sure Billy was ok. By Friday, Jeff did not wait for Billy. He just recited his affirmations and walked to school alone. Jeff's friends had not come outside to help save the world in weeks, nor did they want to play anything other than that stupid video game during lunch or recess. Ever since Hines sent the video game to their classmates, it had consumed all of their attention. They stood around with earbuds hanging from their heads, eyes fixated on their screens while talking to one another about the video game.

"Wait a minute!" Jeff thought. He recalled during recess one of his classmates walking up to Hines to look at a piece of paper he was holding. "Why is everyone hanging around Hines all of a sudden? What's on that paper?" Jeff pondered. Jeff decided to go see what the big fuss was all about.

During lunch, as Jeff dribbled the basketball, he passed a crowd of kids near the basketball court. He saw Phil and Billy. "Hey, Billy! What's up, Phil? What are you all looking at?" Jeff asked.

"Hey, Jeff," Phil replied.

"What are you..." Jeff began to repeat.

"Don't tell Jeff, ha haha," a girl interrupted Phil.

"Yeah, Jeff's the enemy!" a different boy yelled.

"Ha! Ha! Ha!" All of the kids laughed.

Just then, Hines looked up and noticed Jeff in the crowd. He quickly folded the papers and stuck them in his back pocket. "What do you want?" Hines blurted out in Jeff's direction. The crowd of kids parted to reveal Hines in the middle.

"I was not talking to you, Redgrave!" Jeff fired back.

"Only the cool kids play this game, so beat it, you bum!" Hines said. The crowd quickly dispersed as a teacher approached to investigate all of the commotions.

Jeff was left standing alone.

"Is everything OK, Jeff?" Maria asked.

"Yes, ma'am," Jeff answered as he dribbled toward the basket. Maria walked with Jeff still concerned because Jeff did not have his usual smile on his face.

Phil caught up with him. "Hey, Jeff. Are you OK?"

"Yeah, I'm A-OK," Jeff replied, still walking with his head down. "Wanna come by later? Jeff asked Phil reluctantly as he looked up to make eye contact with Phil.

"I already told Billy and Hines I would come by to play the Revenge of the Talking Televisions. You should come too," Phil suggested.

"Huh...No...I'll just see you around," Jeff replied, disappointed that he even asked. He had predicted how Phil would respond.

Phil placed the earbuds back in both ears and retreated back to the crowd

"Are you sure you ok, Jeff?" Maria asked.

"It's that stupid game. It seems like that's all everyone cares about now. You probably play it too!" Jeff snapped at Maria.

"Do you see me playing the game? Maria clapped back. "I am standing here talking to you." Jeff sensed that he offended Maria.

"I'm sorry. I did not mean it like that. It just seems like none of my friends wants to talk to me anymore. I just don't understand."

"There is something fishy about that game. That is why I don't play it."

Yeah, I think so too. I just don'tknow what."

"I can help you get to the bottom of it. You know how I like to solve mysteries!" Maria reminded Jeff of one of her favorite things to do. "Kids in my class are always talking about that game. I will see what I can find out for ya."

"Thanks Maria." Maria seemed to restore any glimmer of hope that Jeff had in his friends, even if it was temporary.

Later that afternoon as Jeff walked home from school he timed how long he could spin the basketball on one finger. He noticed a crowd of kids walking in front of him. They typically kept straight, but today they turned down his street. It was unusual to see that many kids were walking down his street. His eyes widened with anticipation as they approached his driveway. However, they continued, passed his house and stopped at Billy's house. He noticed Phil in the group, as well as all of the other kids who used to come out and pretend to save the world with them. Phil looked back when he heard the bounce of a basketball. Phil waved at Jeff, motioning for him to join them. Hines noticed and discreetly wrapped his arm around Phil's shoulders to guide him into Billy's house. Hines gave Jeff the side-eye as he looked back over his right shoulder just before entering Billy's house. Seeing all of his classmates playing with Billy and Hines made Jeff have a multitude of feelings; some of the feelings were unfamiliar to him. Although he was happy that Billy had new friends, it made him sad that his friends were no longer hanging out with him. Initially, he did not understand why he did not want to go to Billy's house, but he conceded that it was because he knew Redgrave would be there. Jeff no longer wanted to play basketball, so he went inside.

As Jeff sat on his bed reflecting about his newfound feeling of loneliness, tears began to form in his eyes. "Why am I crying?" he thought. As he went to his desk to grab a tissue, he remembered his mother saying, "If you ever have strong feelings about something but you do not want to talk to me or your dad about it, don't hold it in, because that can make you sick. Write it down. Get it out, and it will make you feel better." Jeff grabbed his journal and began to write more about *Super Pencil*. The more Jeff wrote, the less he thought about Redgrave and the better he felt.

Every day after school, Jeff would either journal about his feelings or add to the *Super Pencil* saga. He remembered his dad's offer to help him write, but for now, writing alone was making him feel better. While writing, occasionally he would get an urge to continue his sleuth work to figure out what that video game was about, but he did not know where to start. "What's so special about this video game? I have played video games before, but it is like they can't help themselves." Jeff thought.

The next morning as Jeff walked into the school, Maria tapped Jeff on the shoulder.

"Hey Jeff." Maria whispered as she slid something into his jacket pocket. She tapped the outside of his pocket and said, "For your eyes only." Maria quickened her pace to walk in front of Jeff as if she did not just interact with him. The exchange happened so fast that Jeff was still processing it all.

"Ok. Thanks?" Jeff reached into his pocket to feel what Maria had just placed in there. It felt like a small rectangle. "What is this?" It felt thinker, almost like a piece of cloth folded several times. Jeff could not resist, so he pulled it partly out of his pocket to take a look. "Clues" was written in red across the top of folder pink paper; very nice paper. Jeff detoured to the bathroom, found an empty stall, closed and locked the door behind him. He carefully unfolded the paper, noticing the ruffled edges. "Where did she get paper like this from?" Jeff thought as he finally unfolded it completely. Maria had written four clues on the paper.

1. "Hines and Billy know a lot about the game. They give other kids tips on how to defeat the Big Bad Boss."

2. "Kids are giving Hines their cell phone numbers. He writes them on a piece of paper and puts the paper in his back pocket."

3. "Everyone is going to Billy's house to play the game one day soon."

4. "Something about a Tournament."

Jeff copied the clues that Maria provided into his journal when he got home. These were the first clues that he logged. Whenever he thought of a clue or received a new set of clues from Maria, he would write them in his journal. Every couple of days he read over his clues to see if he could connect any dots.

Chapter 8

Super Pencil!

It was a brilliantly sunny Saturday morning. The skies were blue, and the birds were chirping. Jeff had just gotten out of the shower when he heard lots of voices coming from outside, in front of his house. "Are my friends outside playing already?" He threw on basketball shorts and ran downstairs. He pressed the garage door opener, and the door seemed to take an eternity to open. Jeff ducked and ran under the door before it completely opened, but no one was there. Just then, Jeff heard a few laughs in the distance. As he turned and looked down the street toward Billy's house, he saw a group of kids walking up Billy's driveway. Jeff dropped his head with disappointment and walked back toward the garage.

As Jeff walked back to the garage, his dad was coming out of the house, putting on work gloves. "I thought I heard your friends?" Jeff's dad asked.

"Yeah, they are all over Billy's house, probably playing that stupid game." Jeff pointed toward the window where he could see the silhouette of kids in Billy's bedroom.

Jeff's dad heard the disappointment in his voice. "Why don't you go by and see if Billy will allow you to play as well?" Jeff's dad suggested.

"I'm OK. I'd rather just play catch with you."

Jeff's dad knew there was a deeper reason why Jeff did not want to go over Billy's house, but the thought that his son would rather toss the football with him warmed his heart. With middle school only a couple of months away, he knew that could change quickly, so he did not press Jeff about going to play video games. Jeff's dad took off his work gloves and grabbed the football. "Go long!" Jeff's dad yelled before flinging the football in Jeff's direction.

After thirty minutes, Jeff's mom yelled through the window, "Breakfast is ready!" Jeff was imagining himself in the middle of a big game and had just caught his third touchdown pass to tie the game, so he was not ready to go in.

"Let's go, son, we do not want our breakfast to get cold," Mr. Whitman said. Jeff tossed the ball in the air then ran ahead and caught it. "Touchdown!" Jeff yelled. "J. Whit. catches the game winner for the championship!" Jeff threw the football in the corner, closed the garage, went to wash his hands before breakfast.

"We should talk to him about math and science camp this summer." Mrs. Whitman said to Mr. Whitman as he set the table.

"I guess you're right. Summer will be here before you know it."

"Do you think he will like the camp?" Mrs. Whitman asked.

"The last time we mentioned it, he said it sounded like school in the summer." Mr. and Mrs. Whitman laughed out loud. "It will not compare to the play-all-day camp that he is used to, but we have to do what's best and what prepares him for the future."

"Ok. You tell him when he comes downstairs." Mrs. Whitman said.

"Why do I gotta tell him?" they both laughed again as Jeff sat at the table.

"Hey homie, remember that new camp we were talking to you about? The one where you can learn how to make robots, your own video games, and do science experiments?" Mr. Whitman tried to pick out all of the features that sounded like fun.

"Yeah. I remember. The one that sounded like school over the summer? I still think I need a vacation!" Jeff replied as his parents tried to hold in their laughs.

"Yep. That's the one. We know that you love language arts, but we think this will help you with math. You like science." Mr. Whitman replied.

"I like science, but not like that." Jeff appreciated his parents allowing him to express how he felt, but ultimately he knew they would urge him to do what was in his best interest.

"We will just try it for this summer. If you don't like it, we can try something different next summer." Mrs. Whitman chimed in.

"Besides, we do something fun all the time. You don't need camp for that. You will have a week off from school, then camp will start." Mr. Whitman concluded.

As Jeff helped clear the table, he wondered what he would do for the rest of the day. "Billy's probably playing that game and Phil can't ever come over." Jeff thought. So he went to his room and pulled out his journal. Jeff's love for writing helped him cope with the fact that he had been feeling a little lonely since all of his friends started hanging out with Billy and Hines. Although playing catch with his dad had distracted him, Jeff wanted to journal about how it made him feel to see all of his friends going to Billy's house, even on a Saturday morning. Jeff still suspected something sinister was behind why, all of a sudden, his friends no longer came outside to save the world with him. Now, they preferred to stay inside and play the Revenge of the Talking Televisions with Hines and Billy.

Jeff and Maria sustained their sleuth work through the end of the school year. The fancy paper notes from Maria were pilling up.

He copied her clues into his journal and kept all of her notes in a shoebox that he slid under his bed. Maria was the only one Jeff talked to about his hunches because if he were wrong, it would implicate some of his friends and make them look guilty. Even his interactions with Maria were not normal. She had mastered the art of discreetly passing him more clues. Sometimes he would find them in his desk or in his backpack and he had no idea when Maria left them there. Jeff needed an ally and Maria was perfectly positioned in the same class with the one person who he thought could be an enemy.

1. "Hines goes to program on weekends to learn how to make video games."

2. "Hines invited Billy to come to the program on weekends."

"Every clue that Maria provided has something to do with Hines. I know he has something to do with this?" Jeff thought after sneaking into the bathroom to read another one of Maria's clues. "But that still does not explain why my friends no longer want to hang out with me?" Jeff did not understand what made this game so different. There were several video games, some they even talked about before and after saving the world with Jeff. "What makes this game different?"

It was the last week of school before summer vacation. Although he had not had consistent conversations with Maria, Jeff looked forward to catching eye contact with Maria as they walked down the hallway or from across the lunchroom. "Will I see her over the summer?" Jeff thought as he watched Maria talk with her friends. Jeff was sitting with other classmates, but he still felt alone. None of them was talking to the other. They all had earbuds in their ears when their eyes locked on their screens. Being an only child helped Jeff cope with his friends being distracted by that video game. He knew how to entertain himself.

Jeff still talked sporadically to Billy, Phil, and his other classmates who used to hang out with him, and they were still nice to him. However, their preoccupation with that video game prevented them from participating in the fun they had previously enjoyed with Jeff. He did not want to ruin the chance of them becoming good friends again, so he decided to keep it all to himself—at least until he had proof that Hines was behind this whole conspiracy!

"Come on, Jeff, connect the dots," Jeff mumbled to himself when he got home from school and sat on his bed reviewing the log of dates and times for each clue he and Maria discovered. He listed the names of his classmates who were associated with each clue. He felt like he was close to a big break in his case.

"I heard Jake say that Hines was the designer of the video game. Hines as the designer?" Jeff frowned. "I did not think he had a brain in the big block resting on his shoulders. If Hines had anything to do with this video game, then certainly that could be why my friends no longer want to play with me." Jeff continued to muse over his notes. "They have all played other video games in the past, but they never stopped talking to me because of it. Hmm." Jeff closed his journal, leaving it sitting on the bed.

Jeff grabbed a few of his action figures and reenacted a scene from the Super Pencil comic book he was writing. This would help jump-start his imagination to continue writing his epic saga. Jeff's dad walked past his room and saw him darting from one side of the room to the other with an action figure in each hand, arms extended above his head.

"What battle are you waging today?" Jeff's dad asked. Jeff's dad noticed the journal sitting on the end of the bed. He entered and sat down on Jeff's bed. Jeff continued his epic battle as if he had not even noticed his dad enter the room; he did not even make eye contact with his dad. His dad picked up the journal, flipped to the last page with writing on it, and began to read. He realized that the words on this page corresponded with the saga Jeff was playing out right in front of him. Jeff's dad flipped back through the pages and saw how much Jeff had already written. It was amazing!

"I did not realize you kept going without me. How long have you been writing this?" Jeff's dad asked feeling guilty because he realized how long it had been since he and Jeff wrote together, as promised. For some reason, that question got Jeff's attention. Slightly embarrassed, he walked over and reached for his journal.

"Son, this is really, really good!" Jeff's dad kept looking through the pages. Jeff was delighted by his dad's compliment.

"Tell me what happens next?" Jeff's dad asked.

Jeff's excitement returned as he became engrossed in the battle with the action figures. As he described the next scene in the story, his dad began to write in the pages of his journal. Before they realized it, they had written over ten pages of the story. Jeff was so engaged with his action figures that he did not realize that his father was writing down what he was saying. Jeff's dad showed him the journal. As Jeff read it, he was shocked that his dad captured the essence of everything he had been saying. This reminded Jeff of when he and his friends would write stories and then act them out.

For the next week, Jeff asked his dad to write down the details of the epic saga as he battled with his action figures. Jeff's dad enjoyed the time they spent together, and it appeared to make Jeff feel better about not having friends to play with outside. *Super Pencil* was no longer just a story: it was quality time that cemented a bond for the father while healing the wounds of the son.

Chapter 9

Jeff Meets Joel

"What excites you most about this new math and science camp?" Mr. Whitman asked as they drove to his first day of camp. Jeff paused, tilting his head to the side. He still had mixed emotions. He really enjoyed his previous summer camp. Jeff stared out the passenger-side window, contemplating for a few seconds. He realized that he had relished his former summer camp because of all of his classmates being there, even though he had not hung out with any of them lately.

"I could meet new friends at this camp." Jeff finally answered with anticipation. "Yeah, that's it. I will have a chance to meet new friends," Jeff repeated, but this time he was not as confident in his response.

His dad sensed his uneasiness but did not want to add to his anxiety by asking additional questions, so he just affirmed Jeff's statement. "Yes, you will meet new friends."

The math and science camp was composed of students from schools who lived in the neighborhoods surrounding the community center where the camp was held. Jeff was surprised to see a few familiar faces. Some of the students went to his school, and others he recognized from his former summer camp. Jeff was an extrovert by nature, so it only took him a few minutes to make a connection with a few other students.

During the first activity, the kids were broken into groups of five. They were instructed to tell the group their names, grades, and the schools they attended. After they finished, Jeff's group talked among themselves while the other groups continued.

"What's Up, Jeff!" Joel greeted.

"Good Morning, sir! Joel, right?" Jeff's had trouble maintaining eye contact with Joel. He was focused on his hair that draped almost to his shoulders. Each strand looked like yarn. Jeff thought it was pretty cool. He wondered if his hard could even do that.

"Yeah. Didn't you say you went to the Wheatland's?" Joel asked, wondering why Jeff addressed him as "sir."

"Yes sir!" Jeff responded.

"Yo, why you callin' me sir?" Joel asked then laughed. "Whateva, man. My cousin goes to dat skool. I heard some kid named Hines made a game that got y'all actin' all thirsty? No shade, but the graphics look lame if you ask me. Anyway, it made me think of you 'cause cuzzo kept saying 'Jeff sucks!' I hope he not throwin' shade at you?" Joel giggled.

Jeff's eyes glazed over and his mouth hung open when he heard Joel mention that video game. "Oh no!" Jeff lamented to himself. "This can't be happening! Does everyone in the world know about this stupid game? But, wait. Joel said Hines made the game." Jeff made a mental note to write in his journal later.

Just then, the camp counselor interrupted their conversation. It was time to move on to the next activity. Jeff tried to ignore what just happened, but how he felt was written all over his face.

"So dis yo first time at a camp like this?" Joel asked Jeff.

"Yeah, my parents made me come."

"I didn't want to come either. But my parents said I was good with numbers and liked computers, so they made me come too. Now, it's cool. I won a gold medal at the national competition the last couple years. It's fun and stuff. We go to Disney World. You'll get used to it."

He and Joel were in the same groups for the rest of the day. Before long, Jeff was able to forget about the video game and just enjoy his time with Joel. For the remainder of the week, Jeff and Joel were partners in their projects and activities. "Crack the

Code" was Jeff's favorite activity of the day. During this activity, the camp counselor talked about how computers have a language of their own. The goal was to figure out the math problems to determine which numbers were associated with the letters that were written on the board. The group who finished first won a snack and was able to go to the gym first. This incorporated several things that Jeff loved. He imaged that he needed to crack the code before the bomb blew up the entire world. And the prize was food and basketball time, Game on! Jeff and Joel finished first every day. They were such kindred spirits that it was like they had been friends forever. It seemed like divine intervention that Jeff and Joel were paired with each other day after day.

"So, how was your first week of camp?" Mrs. Whitman asked as Jeff got in the car after camp on Friday.

"It was great!" Jeff said with a jovial tone.

"What made it so great ?" she asked further.

"I met new friends," Jeff answered.

"Who?" Jeff's mom inquired.

"Joel. He's cool," Jeff replied.

"Anyone else?"

"Nope. Just Joel!" Jeff responded.

Jeff was eager to go to camp Monday morning. He was dressed and already sitting in the car when Jeff's dad walked into the garage. Jeff's parents were ecstatic to see Jeff cheerful and excited. They did not expect him to love math and science camp this much.

On Monday, Jeff jumped out of the car and ran into the community center, barely saying goodbye to his dad. Mr. Whitman followed behind him with long strides, trying to keep up. In his peripheral view, Jeff's dad could see Jeff and Joel greeting each other with a barrage of hand smacks, waves, and fist bumps. "Special handshake already. That's a good sign," Jeff's dad thought.

"See you later, Big Homie!" Jeff rushed over hugged his father and Joel followed behind him.

"My cousin was playing that dumb game all weekend. It killed me every time he said 'Jeff sucks!' I guess you gotta say that to get someone on yo squad to give you a life."

Mr. Whitman overheard what Joel said to Jeff as he signed Jeff in, but dismissed it, not knowing what he was really referring to.

"I would always say, 'Not all Jeffs' 'cause the one I know is pretty cool," Joel explained. "It must be hard sayin' 'you suck' while playin' dat game, huh?" Joel asked.

"I've never played it," Jeff replied.

"What? Never? I thought errbody at da Wheatlands was addicted to dat garbage," Joel expressed. "I know you were salty hearing 'Jeff sucks' all day, errday at school?" Joel gave Jeff a sympathetic look. "Errtime I go to my cousin's crib da only thang he wants to do is sit 'round and play dat damn game. We used to go outside, hoop, and ride our bikes, but nooooo—not since Revenge of the whateva-you-call-it. It's like he brainwashed or somethin'." Joel pulled a chair from the table to sit down.

Jeff was delighted that someone finally understood how he had been feeling, even though he had kept those feelings locked inside. "It was cool. I knew they were not talking about me," Jeff casually replied. Jeff still did not have the courage to admit to himself or anyone else that he had been feeling isolated and lonely since everyone started playing that game. Hearing "Jeff sucks" all day did not make it any better.

"Brainwashed?" Jeff said with a giggle as he made a mental note for his journal once he got home.

"Take me to yo leader!" Joel replied in a robot voice while making stiff, jerky robot-like motions with his arms. They both bursted out laughing as they walked into the gym.

"Pair up. Today we are going to the Computer Lab." a camp counselor prepared the students for the next activity.

"Yo. Dis is Dope! You will like da Lab." Joel jumped up and stood by the door. He turned and saw Jeff still sitting at the table. "Yo!" Joel signaled for Jeff to come to the door with him. When Jeff walked up, Joel explained. "We have to be first to get a good computer. Some of em wack. They way too slow for what imma show you." Joel ran over to the last row of computers. Where they were sitting, the camp counselor could not see their screen.

This allowed Joel time to play or work on one of his apps without being noticed. After his first year at the camp, Joel searched the Internet and taught himself more about coding and creating apps and video games. "This is like my computer at home. It was one of da prizes when I won wit my first gold medal for codin'a couple years ago." Jeff could not believe his eyes. The game on the screen looked like one that was purchased from the store.

"That pretty cool." Jeff said. "Did you build this game yourself?"

"Yes Sir! This is all me."

"Did you learn how to do this in this camp?"

"What! Well, they gave me the appetite, but I had to learn how to eat myself."

Jeff was impressed. The idea of creating his own video game intrigued him, but he was more proud at the thought of Joel being able to do it than with him having the possibility to learn how to. He loved to write super sagas, pretend to save the world, and shoot hoops.

As Joel whispered about the features of the game and what coding language and equipment needed to enhance the features, Jeff was checking out Joel's new kicks.

"Nice shoes! Those new?" Jeff asked.

"Bro! Are you even listening to me? I'm trying to school you."

"Yeah. Yeah. Keep going." Within seconds, Jeff began to imagine how to finish his Super Pencil epic saga.

"...and that is why Revenge of the whateva-you-call-it is so wack." That statement got Jeff's attention, but he had not been listening.

"You understand now?" Joel saw the blank look on Jeff's face so he kept typing.

Joel and Jeff created a bond that was very strong.

Chapter 10

The Plot Thickens

Lately, Hines had become more irritated by Billy's corniness. Hines's motivation for hanging out with Billy was primarily because he had noticed that Billy and Jeff were friends. Hines could not resist the opportunity to drive a wedge between Jeff and anyone who was his friend. Besides, Billy lived a few houses down from Jeff. This gave Hines the opportunity to spy on Jeff without Jeff being suspicious about why he was on his street. Hines had not seen kids playing at Jeff's house all summer. This made Hines very excited. It appeared that his plot to take all of Jeff's friends was actually working.

Jeff's birthday was July 5. The Fourth of July holiday was a time when Jeff's parents planned an epic birthday bash that all the kids in the neighborhood enjoyed. Hines had been working on a newer version of his game since many of his classmates had completed all of the levels. Hines planned to debut his game with a Fourth of July tournament. He had been saving his allowance and the money he made from in-app purchases to offer a *big* prize for the winner of the tourney. He remembered that many of his classmates eagerly anticipated the annual epic birthday bash at Jeff's house. Therefore, Hines planned the timing of the tournament to disrupt Jeff's epic birthday celebration. Hines figured that if the kids enjoyed themselves at Jeff's as they had in years past, he might lose the momentum gained with the Revenge of the Talking Televisions. Hines's programming skills had improved due to extra studying and his experience with the last game. He no longer required help from his older brother to complete the newer version of the game. The updates to the game still included subliminal messages, and he made them appear even more frequently than in the previous version. He slightly improved the graphics and features of the Big Bad Boss. He wanted to install more improvements, but the epic birthday bash was around the corner. He did not want to miss his opportunity to steal all of Jeff's friends once and for all.

Hines heard that Jeff had been snooping around and asking questions about the game. So one day, while at Billy's house, Hines hacked into the Wi-Fi at Jeff's house. He recorded his IP address and blocked it within his video games app. If Jeff ever got ahold of the link to download the game, it would not work once the game recognized Jeff's IP address.

As Hines was preparing to send out the invitations to the tournament, he thought about the sad look Jeff would have on his face when no one showed up to his little birthday bash. He did not want to miss that occasion. "I got it!" Hines exclaimed. "I will ask Billy to host the tournament. That way, Jeff will see all of his friends coming to the tourney instead of his kiddie party. I will be there to witness it all."

Hines ran downstairs to ask his mother to call Billy's parents. Hines's mother instantly agreed with his idea. She was excited that he had found something that he was passionate about; however, she was not aware of his misguided motivations behind the game. Hines stood at his mother's side while she called Mrs. Ramirez. They discussed logistics for a while, but both were thrilled to support the efforts of their sons. After Mrs. Ramirez agreed to host the tournament, Hines rushed upstairs to send the invitation to all the people who had already downloaded his game. He also sent a text and direct message with the invitation for the tournament, which included a free link to the updated version of the game once they RSVPed. He sent it to all of the third-, fourth-, and fifth-grade students at the Wheatlands. Hines was in charge of sending the invites. That way, no one would notice that Jeff's name was left off the list.

Epic Planning

Mrs. Whitman did not understand why he was not excited about his epic birthday bash this year. Jeff's mom loved to host events, and Jeff loved to have friends over. Planning this epic birthday bash allowed her and Jeff to spend some quality time together. However, Jeff was not as engaged as in previous years. She stopped at the doorway to Jeff's room and leaned against the doorframe. Jeff was lying across his bed, writing in his journal.

"Jeff, are there any new friends that you would like to invite this year?" She asked, trying to engage him.

"No," Jeff replied, sounding irritated with her question.

"What about Billy and his sister? This would be their first time attending."

Jeff shrugged his shoulders as to say he did not care if they came or not and continued to write in his journal.

Jeff's mom started to get a little irritated by Jeff's nonchalant attitude. Jeff's responses were almost rude; however, she did not react. Jeff's erratic mood swings caused her to be more concerned than upset. It was out of character for Jeff to act this way toward her. She walked away to find Jeff's dad sitting at his desk. They discussed Jeff's recent behavior and did not understand why in the mornings he appeared happy, then after camp he seemed a little depressed. They concluded there had to be a correlation to him no longer playing with friends once he got home from camp.

"Could it be that he is not excited because he does not think his friends will come?" Mrs. Whitman's eye lit up. "I have an idea!" she said as she walked away.

Jeff's mom had not sent formal invitations in years. However, this year she decided to send an electronic invite to the parents of

Jeff's friends who had attended in previous years. She wanted to confirm they were coming. She figured that if she was able to tell Jeff who was coming, he might become more excited about the epic birthday bash.

After a couple of days, Jeff's mom noticed more declines than in previous years. She expected some, but when she received regrets from those who had made this event an annual tradition for their family, she thought it was odd. By the end of the week, more than half of the families declined the invitation, and most of the others responded with "maybe." Jeff's mom was really disappointed. She sent a few text messages to the parents to figure out why so many people were declining.

Mrs. Whitman received a reply from Mrs. Parker. "Phil said there is a big video game tournament that day. Tried to convince him, but he said big prizes. It is actually on your street."

"On my street?" Jeff's mom asked in her reply to the text. She had no time to waste. If kids did not show up to Jeff's party, she knew that would crush him. His spirits were already low, so she did not want him to drop into depression. She had to think fast!

"Jeff, who are some of your friends at math and science camp?" Jeff's mom asked as she burst into his room.

She'd startled him. "Uh…ummm…the kids there are really nice. I have made a lot of friends. They even voted me the section leader this week." Then Jeff added, more excitedly, "Joel for sure! And there is…" Jeff began to call out the names of all of the kids who were in his section.

"That's it! His camp section!" Jeff's mom thought with anticipation. "OK, thanks!" His mother said as she ran out of his room. She grabbed her laptop and looked through her e-mails to find the welcome packet that the math and science camp had sent. A parent contact list was included so that parents could connect when their kids were completing group projects. She sent the invitation to all of the families in Jeff's camp section. She also included some of the families from Jeff's youth group at church. She hoped and prayed that some of them would be available to attend Jeff's party, even though it was a holiday weekend and was not a tradition for those families.

Within minutes, she began to receive confirmations. Her eyes widened with excitement as she heard all of the notifications indicating she was receiving new text messages. By the next day, most of the kids from Jeff's math and science camp had confirmed their attendance.

"Wow. If they all come, this could be even bigger than in years past," Mrs. Whitman contemplated. She could not contain her enthusiasm. She had to start planning right away! Mrs. Whitman jumped up from the couch and made a mad dash for her SUV as she shouted to her husband, "Be right back, honey! I am running to the store to pick up a couple things for the party!"

***

It was a warm sunny summer morning. The birds were singing outside Jeff's bedroom window, a welcoming sound for him to wake up to a new day. The sunlight shined through the cracks of his window blinds, creating stripes of shade and sun on his wall and basketball trophies. A stripe of sunlight crossed Jeff's face and woke him. Jeff lay in bed for a few minutes reminiscing about being outside, saving the world with his friends.

After washing his face and brushing his teeth, Jeff grabbed his basketball and went outside to play. Jeff heard the sound of a garage door rising between the beats of his ball bouncing off the pavement. That sound usually made Jeff excited because it typically meant that one of his friends was coming to join him. He glanced up and down the street until he saw Billy emerge from his garage. "Is he coming down here to play?" Jeff thought. Billy continued down the sidewalk and stopped when he got to Jeff's driveway.

"Hi, Jeff," Billy said. At this moment, Billy realized that he had not spoken to Jeff in quite a while. He felt a little embarrassed, given that Jeff was his first friend in the whole neighborhood. Jeff had even introduced him to many of the classmates he now hung out with. "Why haven't I talked to Jeff in so long?" Billy thought. Billy had a flashback of all of the fun they used to have, and it brought a smile to his face. After an awkward silence, Jeff's greeting interrupted Billy's daydreaming.

"Hey, Billy!" Jeff said, trying to hold back the excitement of having a friend over.

"My mom and dad wanted me to see if you were coming to the ROT3 tournament in a few weeks?" Billy asked in a monotone voice, feeling confused about why the thought "Don't talk to Jeff" was running through his mind.

"Rock3? What's that?" Jeff asked.

"No, ROT3. You know, the Revenge of the Talking Televisions—the video game? The name was too long, so Hines made it an acronym. I know you do not really like video games that much, but..."

"*Aha!*" Jeff thought. "So Hines *is* behind this dumb game." He continued to connect the dots and make mental notes to write in his journal when he would be inside. "When is the tournament?" Jeff asked, trying to be cordial.

"July fourth at five p.m. Hines said that all of our classmates have already said they are coming, so you should come too," Billy replied.

"That is the same day as..." Jeff slowly mumbled, then stopped because he then knew that meant no one was coming to his epic birthday bash. "I will check with my parents and let you know," Jeff said as he looked down.

"OK, see ya," Billy replied as he ran back toward his home, relieved that the conversation was over.

Jeff hurried into the house to log more clues in his journal, but he could not help thinking about the fact that all of his friends were going to be at the ROT3 tournament and he was not even invited. As he recalled his conversation with Billy, he also determined that Billy probably only invited him because his parents told him to.

Jeff's Journal Entries

#1 ROT3 is an acronym for Revenge of the Talking Televisions

#2 Hines named the game ROT3

#3 Hines is helping plan the ROT3 tournament, July 5 at 5:00 p.m., at Billy's house.

#4 How did everyone know about the tournament except for me?

Later that night, after Jeff had taken a shower, he walked slowly into his parents' room and knelt down at his mother's side of the bed. "Mom, I would be OK if…if we did not have the party this year," Jeff expressed with sadness.

"But, Jeff, we have been doing this for years now, and you always have so much fun. What makes this year different?" Jeff's mom inquired.

Jeff paused. "I am just not sure if any of my friends will actually come," he finally replied.

"But Jeff, why would you think that?" Jeff's mom probed, already knowing the answer.

Jeff paused again. "Billy told me that they are having a ROT3 tournament at his house, on July fourth, and that all of the kids are going over there. I know they want me to rot! I hate that stupid game!" Tears began streaming down his face.

"Wait, what? Slow down, Jeff, slow down," Jeff's parents said at the same time. They sat up on the bed, dropped to the floor, and wrapped their arms around Jeff to console him.

"What is a Rot Tree?" Mr. Whitman asked in a whisper. "What is a Rot Tree?" he asked again when Jeff didn't answer right away.

"No, Dad! ROT3. It's an acronym for that dumb game, Revenge of the Talking Televisions," Jeff explained.

Jeff's parents quickly made eye contact when they heard Jeff mention the game again.

"I knew Hines had something to do with it. No one wants to be my friend anymore. They rather play that dumb game, call me names, and laugh at me!" Jeff said through his tears.

"Jeff, we discussed this before. It's only a game. Jeff is a common name and…"

"No!" Jeff interrupted. "I have been taking notes, and I think I have enough evidence that Hines is behind all of this."

"Hines created an entire video game? Impressive!" Mr. Whitman replied.

"David!" Jeff's mom clapped back to refocus her husband so that he did not appear to be supporting Hines instead of his son.

Mr. Whitman's mouthed "sorry" apologetically.

"But Jeff, you said Hines is trying to steal your friends. Do you have proof of that too?" Mrs. Whitman asked, trying to be rational.

"No, but ever since our fight in summer camp he swore he would get revenge!"

"Fight? Wait, what fight?" Mrs. Whitman's demeanor shifted, and she quickly stood up. Jeff's head had been resting on her shoulder, so he hit his head on the side of the bed as he fell to the floor. "I'm calling his mother right now!" Jeff's mom exclaimed.

"Liz!" Mr. Whitman grabbed his wife by the thigh to prevent her from making the phone call. She sat back down, realizing that she had dropped Jeff in her moment of fury. "You OK, baby?"

Still looking down, Jeff was so distraught that he did not notice his parents bickering. Jeff sat up and rested his back on the bed before continuing, "The fight happened a couple years ago in summer camp..."

"A couple years ago!" Jeff's mom tried to jump up again, knocking Jeff over again. Mr. Whitman grabbed her and motioned for her to calm down and allow Jeff to finish.

"No one likes me anymore, Mom. Please cancel the party!" Jeff pleaded as he looked at his mother directly in her eyes and then covered his face with both hands. His palms were now soaking wet from his tears. Jeff could not believe that he had finally said out loud what he had been thinking for months. Although he did not like to cry, especially in front of anyone, he instantly felt better after telling his parents how he had been feeling. He did not go into the level of detail that he had written in his journal, but simply voicing his thoughts made him feel as if a boulder had been lifted off his chest. He could finally breathe again.

Mr. and Mrs. Whitman were devastated to see how hurt their son was and to think it started over a year ago. The emotions of the moment overwhelmed them, and they began to tear up as well. It hurt them to see their son struggle with friendships and self-esteem, especially because they both had appeared to be areas of strength for Jeff. They experienced many mixed emotions: anger because the summer camp never told them about a fight that occurred more than a year ago, sadness because their son had been wrestling with these emotions for so long on his own, and frustration because they felt powerless against how it was impacting him.

Mr. Whitman hugged Jeff and began whispering in his ear, "Jeff, you are more than a conqueror. No weapon formed against you will prosper. Greater is the one who lives inside of you than those in the world. You can do all things through Christ who strengthens you!"

Jeff immediately calmed down. Ever since he was a little boy, his father's voice had always seemed to have a calming effect on him. It soothed him and made him feel safe. Even when Jeff was in trouble, his dad never raised his voice. The tone and inflection of his dad's voice would change based on the mood and tone of the conversation, but he never yelled at Jeff.

The words that his dad whispered sounded familiar to him. Hearing his dad's voice caused something to wake up inside of him. The power of those words helped Jeff to refocus on what could be, instead of how he felt in this moment. Jeff had flashbacks of his father saying, *"It does not matter what others think of you. It matters most what you think of yourself. It only hurts you when people say false and bad things about you if you believe them to be true. God made you special and no one else can change that!"*

Jeff knew that everything would be OK. At that moment, Jeff decided he was *not* going to allow that dumb video game to consume his thoughts any longer. Allowing the game to consume his thoughts caused an adjustment in his attitude, which impacted how he interacted with his family and friends.

"No more!" Jeff said to himself with conviction. Now more than ever, he was sure that dumb video game was the root cause of the dissension between him and his friends. Jeff settled on his action plan, thinking, "I am going to prove it and get things back to how they used to be." Suddenly, Jeff jumped to his feet, gave his mom and dad a big hug, and skipped out of the room as if nothing had happened.

Not understanding the resolution that had just taken place inside of Jeff, his parents looked at each other and shrugged their shoulders in bewilderment.

"What just happened?" Jeff's dad asked. He was confused that Jeff could be so emotionally distraught in one moment and minutes later skip out of their room as if nothing happened. "Well, amen!" Mr. Whitman said.

Mrs. Whitman wiped the tears from her face. They sat there for a bit longer, silently processing what they had experienced and heard from their son and how it made them feel. They had never experienced such raw emotion from their son and, actually, it freaked them out a little. What seemed small to them was actually monumental to Jeff.

So many questions began to cross their minds as they replayed their interactions with Jeff over the past several days, weeks, and months. They thought they were very engaging and present in their son's life. However, based on this outburst of emotion, clearly they had overlooked or minimized the warning signs.

"What could we have done differently? Or what can we do now to ensure our son does not have to go through anything like this again in the future, especially alone?" Mr. Whitman thought. He broke the silence. "The fact that all of Jeff's old friends declined the epic birthday bash kinda validates what Jeff was saying."

Mrs. Whitman was still lost in her own thoughts, so she did not acknowledge what her husband had just said. She spoke at last. "It has been months since I have seen Jeff outside playing with other kids. I just figured they were on vacation or something. I should have known." Tears started to stream down her face again.

Mr. Whitman resisted the urge to try to offer a solution in the moment and just embraced his wife to comfort her.

Chapter 11

Don't Worry, Be Happy!

More than a week had passed since Jeff expressed to his parents how he was feeling about his friends, playing alone, and not wanting to have the epic birthday bash this year. Jeff hoped that they had forgotten about his little outburst, so he did not mention it to them and hoped they would do the same. Jeff began to adjust to playing alone by finishing *Super Pencil* with his dad. *Super Pencil* had become the topic of conversation at the dinner table. Jeff would draw pictures of the various characters and create mock-ups for the cover of the book. His dad created a collage on the walls of his office from all of the comic-book covers that Jeff had drawn.

Jeff was so eager to write down the ideas he thought of while at camp that he pulled the car door handle before the car came to a complete stop in the garage. "Jeff!" Mr. Whitman slammed on the breaks to stop the car and grabbed Jeff by the arm stopping him from jumping out a moving car. "It is not safe to open the door until the car has come to a complete stop. Be patient!" The jerk of the car and the force of his dad's hand clenching his bicep startled Jeff.

"Sorry, Dad," Jeff apologized as he jumped out of the car and rushed into the house. As Jeff removed his shoes in the mudroom, he overheard his mother talking on the phone. It sounded like she was ordering food! "Food!" Jeff thought. He was always hungry. Jeff sniffed the air as he removed his left shoe, but he did not smell anything cooking. "Mom must be ordering dinner?" Jeff thought. "That's right, delivery on July fourth," Jeff heard his mom say.

"Ohhhh nooooo! She's still planning my epic birthday bash!" Jeff panicked. "But all of the kids will be down the street with Billy and Hines at the ROT3 tournament! I told them to cancel this thing!" Jeff was flustered.

Jeff went to his room to contemplate how he was going to foil his parent's plans. He knew they were doing this to make him feel better. "Come on, Jeff, think fast." Jeff took a moment to deliberate. "I know! Maybe I could act really happy so they do not think I need the party to make me feel better?" Jeff said to himself as he paced the floor of his bedroom. "Yeah, that's it! They will not feel the urge to have this party just for me." Jeff ran out of his room and down the stairs to the kitchen where his mom and dad were preparing dinner together.

"I am so happy!" Jeff blurted out. "I am the happiest kid on earth! Maybe the entire universe!"

His parents giggled and asked, "Why are you so happy?"

"No particular reason. I am just a happy boy with no complaints in the whole wide world." Jeff repeated this three more times while doing a Michael Jackson kick and a couple of spins in the middle of the kitchen floor. His socks against the hardwood made him spin faster than he expected. *Boom*! Jeff fell to the floor.

"Jeff! Are you OK?" Mrs. Whitman said, reaching to help him up.

"Mom, I am fine. 'Cause, remember, I am so happy!"

"That's your son, and he gets that from your side of the family," Mr. Whitman joked as he exited the kitchen.

Jeff waited around a few minutes to see if it worked. "Are we still having the epic birthday bash?" Jeff inquired.

"Of course! It will be great, just like every year," Jeff's mom responded as she hugged Jeff. Jeff dropped his head and closed his eyes, resting all of his weight on his mom's arms. "Oh No! It did not work!" Jeff thought.

"Jeff! We are going to fall!" Jeff's mom exclaimed as she stumbled forward because of his weight.

"But I said I was already happy." Jeff explained.

"What? Trust me! You will have a great time, as always!" She assured him. Mrs. Whitman knew she had received confirmations from many of his new friends at the math and science camp, and she had even made a few more calls to arrange a surprise guest from his current school.

ROT3 Tourney

Jeff's mom loved to host events. She woke up early, cleaned the house, and finished all of the decorations. She always streamed her favorite music stations while she worked. Music ignited her creative side. She really enjoyed doing all sorts of things to make her family happy.

Jeff stayed in bed longer than usual this day. He lay on his back, staring at the ceiling, with his fingers interlocked behind his head. "Lord, help me!" Jeff prayed. The epic birthday bash was just hours away. Jeff heard a commotion outside his window. He arose to take a look and saw delivery trucks at Billy's house. They were dropping off four enormous screens that had skulls at the top left and right corners. Black and purple balloons lined Billy's driveway leading to the door. A sidewalk artist drew the ROT3 logo on each square in front of the house. Purple and black streamers filled the trees in front of the house. It looked as if someone had "TPed" the house but in a very cool and creative way. A smoke machine was placed behind the shrubs, which created a light haze that covered the front of the house. It was just enough to allow you to see the laser lights that danced to the beat of the music blaring from the backyard. The bass from the music reverberated through Jeff's room. His basketball trophies appeared to dance to the beat, shaking and moving closer to the edge of the shelf with each wave of bass.

Jeff watched as they made the final touches to the tourney decorations. He saw them roll a generator to the side of the house, opposite the path that led to the backyard. Within minutes a wacko-waving-inflatable-arms-man came to life from the middle of the driveway. It had the ROT3 logo across its chest. It seemed to have well-choreographed moves as it gyrated to the beat of the music.

Although he still felt the video game was stupid, Jeff was actually impressed with the level of detail used to decorate the place for the tournament. Jeff scanned the decorations at his own house in contrast to the spectacle a couple of houses away. As Jeff rose to walk away from his bedroom window, he saw two men coming off a ladder on Billy's roof. They had just hung a banner that stretched the entire width of the house. Jeff went to the other window in his room to reposition himself so that he could see what the banner said. Of course, it read "Jeff Sucks!" In weeks past, reading that banner would have made him sad, but not today.

"You may have won this battle, but I will win the war!" Jeff said convincingly, standing firm, with both his fists balled and resting on his hips. He stuck out his chest and locked a brave gaze on that banner.

Just as Jeff started to envision himself ripping that banner off the house and destroying everything that had a ROT3 logo on it, he smelled the fresh aroma of bacon. Jeff's eyes widened, and he made a dash for the kitchen. Food always made Jeff happy, especially bacon!

The Epic Birthday bash

Jeff typically greeted each of his guests as they arrived. He was anxious to see if anyone would come to his party. He recalled the last time he had spoken to Billy, when Billy had told him that all of their classmates had already RSVPed for the ROT3 tournament. Jeff stood in the middle of his driveway, and his heart raced as each car slowly drove down his street. They all passed him and stopped in front of Billy's house. Jeff would wave at the kids he knew as they exited their cars, but the ROT3 lure was too strong. Many of them did not even notice Jeff due to the lights, smoke, and music. After about an hour of watching kids arrive at Billy's down the street, Jeff was overcome with disappointment. Not one kid had come to Jeff's epic birthday bash thus far.

Jeff went into the house and grabbed his journal to begin to log his feelings of defeat. He plopped down on the area rug in the middle of his bedroom. This had become Jeff's favorite spot to write.

"Jeff! It is almost time! Aren't you going to greet your guests like you always do?" His mother said with excitement.

"What guests?" Jeff thought as tears dripped onto the pages of his journal. Just as he placed the pencil to the page to inscribe his current mood—*ding dong*! At the sound of the doorbell Jeff's head whipped upward, and he jumped to his feet, eager to see who was at the door.

Jeff's mouth dropped to the floor when he saw a few of his friends from math and science camp. He looked over their shoulders and could see dozens of his friends from math and science camp walking up the driveway. Jeff looked at his mom with pure joy on his face and then darted out the door to greet his guests. That glance of excitement made Mrs. Whitman's heart melt. She realized that she had not seen him this happy in a long time.

Jeff stood in the driveway and greeted his guests as he had done every year. Mrs. Whitman had already prepared the backyard with several stations: activities, carnival games, a volleyball net, corn hole, crafts, board games, food, and more! There was something to engage everyone who arrived. She also included a lockbox with a sign attached that said "No Phone Zone!" that the kids would pass as they entered the backyard. This was for them to store their phones in, to ensure that all of the kids connected with one another and not their devices. The backyard was beginning to fill; therefore, Mrs. Whitman relieved him of his greeting duties so that he could go have fun with his friends. Jeff quickly bear-hugged his mom. With his head pressed snuggly into her torso, he said, "I love you, Mom," before sprinting for the backyard. That gesture of gratitude from her son put another huge smile on her face and in her heart. Mr. Whitman witnessed it all through the storm door and admired how his wife always knew exactly what to do to please everyone in her family.

Jeff was excited to see Joel. Joel had become one of Jeff's best friends at math and science camp. Jeff rushed over to corn hole and grabbed the white beanbags with the green Michigan State University Spartan logo. Joel was preparing to launch the green ones across the yard into the hole just beneath the green Spartan head.

"Awww, so close!" Jeff yelled from behind Joel.

Joel looked over at his dad to see if he had noticed how close he had come to making it in the hole on the first try, but his parents were engaged in small talk with Jeff's dad. The backyard was quite festive in its decor, and the buzz of kids' voices and laughter as they enjoyed the festivities complemented the scene perfectly.

"Dude, I saw dat banner as we pulled up to yo crib. Whatz up wit dat?" Joel asked Jeff.

"What banner?" Jeff tried to act like he was unaware and unfazed about what Joel was talking about.

"You sayin' you didn't see dat big ole 'Jeff Sucks!' banner hangin' on da house down da street?" Joel stared at Jeff inquisitively. "Dat must be dat stupid tournament my cousin said he was goin' to instead of coming to yo gig."

At that very moment, the distant sound of rock music filled the air. Haze and laser beams danced above the horizon of privacy fences. The familiar reverberation of the music caused a few heads to bob, and some kids even danced to the grooves coming from a few backyards over.

***

Hines was curious to see Jeff's face when no one came to his party. "Hey, Billy, can I get my charger from your room? I left it there the other day," Hines asked.

"Yeah, go ahead," Billy said.

Hines used this as an excuse to look out of Billy's bedroom window to see what was happening at Jeff's house. As he looked out the window, he could see dozens of kids walking up Jeff's driveway, going into his backyard. Jeff was hugging his mother and running behind the other kids. Hines smacked the windowsill and grit his teeth. The force from the smack caused the window to shake. Hines was even more upset because not only did his plan appear to be unraveling, but he had no idea where all these kids had come from. Hines did not recognize any of them, so he knew that they did not attend the Wheatlands.

"You have gotta be kidding me! Where did he get more friends from?" Hines shrieked. He saw them all go into the Jeff's backyard, so he had to think fast.

Hines ran downstairs and into the backyard. He grabbed the mic from the DJ and yelled, "Everyone gets unlimited lives for the first round of the tournament if you repeat after me, 'Jeff sucks!'"

Everyone at the tournament formed a circle around him as they shouted, "Jeff sucks! Jeff sucks! Jeff sucks!" Hines danced, jumping up and down in the middle of the circle, which incited the crowd to do the same.

Hines hoped that Jeff would hear them several doors down, and it worked. The echo of the chant filled the air, but it was not quite loud enough for those in Jeff's backyard to comprehend what was being said. Joel was curious, so he walked over to the fence closest to the sound, which was opposite the patio where their parents were talking.

"What are they saying?" Joel asked others who joined him after seeing him with his ear pressed against the fence.

"Who cares?" Jeff replied.

"Are they saying what I think they are saying?" another kid asked with disgust in his voice.

Just then, Jeff realized what they were saying and tried to hide his emotions.

"Jeff sucks! Jeff sucks! Jeff sucks!" bellowed from the tournament goers, and the chant appeared to be getting louder by the second.

Joel realized that the chant was having a negative impact on Jeff. "Last one to the volleyball net is a meathead!" Joel barked. The net was on the other side of the backyard. Joel wanted to get Jeff as far away from that dissenting energy to ensure he enjoyed his party. The kids followed Joel.

Jeff was super competitive as the volleyball game began. His demeanor shifted as soon as his team scored their first point. "Yeah!" Jeff cheered.

Joel was still distracted. He was now determined to figure out what was going on with this ROT3 video game. Although Jeff did not convey anything to him, Joel suspected this video game was beginning to take its toll on Jeff. "Don't you worry 'bout a thang, Jeff. You my boy. I got yo back."

Several parents joined the game of volleyball with their kids. It was a fun time for everyone. Just as the opposing team was about to serve, Jeff saw the bright glow of a yellow sundress entering the backyard. Jeff could not believe his eyes. It was Maria!

Jeff's mom had run into Maria and her parents at the grocery store a few days ago. She told them about the epic birthday bash. Maria was super excited about the opportunity to come celebrate with Jeff, but they had not RSVPed.

Some of the other boys looked in awe as she gracefully walked through the backyard with her mom, her jet black hair blowing in the wind. It was as if she was moving in slow motion with theme music playing in the background. "Maria is at my house?" Jeff thought as he continued to stare at her. "How did she even know about my party?"

Maria made eye contact with Jeff, and he raised his hand to wave at her. Jeff and Maria shared a warm smile of excitement. Maria was waving back at Jeff rather energetically, but her face seemed worried. *Bam!* The serve smacked Jeff on the side of the head. Maria had actually been trying to warn him about the volleyball zeroing in on his face. One of Jeff's teammates recovered the serve by hitting the ball in the air and in Jeff's direction. Jeff gathered himself and realized he had a chance to redeem this embarrassing moment. He jumped—in his mind, as high as he had ever jumped—and spiked the ball as hard as he ever had with his left hand rising over the net. The ball whizzed past the heads of his opponents as they all yelled, "Out!" But the ball caught the back right corner of the sideline.

"It's in! It's in! We win!" Jeff's team celebrated.

"I meant to do that!" Jeff said with a new swag when he realized that was the game-winning point.

As they got something to drink, Jeff introduced Maria to his friends from math and science camp. Joel and the other boys stared, giggled, and pointed at Jeff as he talked to Maria. Jeff could see them making fun of him over Maria's shoulder, so he tried not to laugh.

"It's great to finally meet Jeff!" Maria's mother said, talking to Jeff's mom. "Jeff this, Jeff that' is all we hear at home."

Jeff's mom repeated the same sentiments.

"Sorry we were late," Maria started. "We went to the wrong house. We saw the sign that said 'Jeff,' but I did not realize it said 'Jeff Sucks.' The tree branches were kinda blocking the entire banner. That is a mean sign." Maria continued, "All the kids play that stupid game, but I don't like it. Some say that the game is not talking about you, but based on our clues, I think Hines did that on purpose." Maria was the only one from Jeff's school who attended his party this year. Jeff blushed, but resisted his natural urge to avoid eye contact with Maria. He wanted to appreciate every moment of having Maria at his house.

Jeff's mom invited the other kids to the cake table. They all surrounded the table and sang happy birthday to Jeff. .

The Fourth of July is synonymous with fireworks, but Jeff was not a fan of fireworks. As a baby, he was sensitive to loud noises; therefore, the unexpected explosive sounds overshadowed the pretty colors and cool effects. It was almost dusk, and several of the kids and parents were still enjoying one another's company. Typically, Jeff's mom ended the epic birthday bash before dark to allow time for everyone to view fireworks elsewhere, but this year everyone seemed to stay longer than usual.

Shrieeeeeeeeek! Everyone turned toward the familiar sound of a firework launching into the air. Jeff covered his ears, because he knew that at the end of that streak of light came an eruption of color and sound. *Boom!* Fireworks lit up the sky. Jeff tried to keep calm as his eyes panned the crowd for his mother. He did not want to appear scared in front of Maria, so he played it cool. The fireworks were coming from the ROT3 tournament. Jeff had been having so much fun at his epic birthday bash that he forgot how irritated he had been just a few hours earlier.

Hines had his parents hire a pyrotechnician to top off the tournament after they announced the winner. As everyone focused on the fireworks, this gave Hines an opportunity to sneak away to see what was happening at Jeff's house. Hines scaled the neighbors' fences and crept through their backyards to peek through the planks in the privacy fence next door to Jeff's house. He was so angry to see all of the kids at Jeff's party. "Who are all these kids?" Hines said as he kicked the base of the fence. No one noticed the noise due to the fireworks blazing above. Hines was infuriated because his plot to take all of Jeff's friends hit a snag, a really *big* snag.

"Just when I thought I had taken them all, he found a whole new squad?" Hines thought with a puzzled look on his face. He knew that the fireworks would be coming to an end soon, so he started hurrying back before anyone realized that he was gone. On the way back, he got too close to the neighbor's house, and the motion detector triggered their back-porch light to come on. "*Roof, roof!*" The dog in the house started barking when he saw Hines running through the backyard. The dog scared Hines so much that he peed his pants. This made him even angrier! He scurried across two more yards and eased back into the crowd of the tournament, just as the fireworks came to an end. Self-conscious about the wet mark on his shorts, Hines pretended to spill punch on his shorts so no one would notice. "Damn you, Jeff

Whitman!" Hines mumbled as he wiped his leg with a paper towel.

"This was such a great time! Thanks for the invite!" parents expressed as they exchanged pleasantries before leaving Jeff's house.

"The fireworks were such a nice surprise. A great way to close out the night," another parent stated.

The parents made more small talk as they walked down the driveway. Jeff still could not believe that Maria was at his house. He ran into the house to grab his smartphone and selfie stick to capture the moment. Though Jeff's mom made the party a "No Phone Zone," when she saw Jeff come out of the house with his phone and selfie stick, she understood why Jeff was breaking this cardinal rule, so she allowed it.

"Selfie!" Jeff screamed as he approached his friends with his selfie stick extended high from his left hand. Jeff, Maria, Joel, and a couple of other kids struck a pose behind Jeff.

After Jeff took the first picture, he noticed that Maria was next to him. He glanced back at Joel and the others with widened eyes and nodded his head to the right, hoping they would take the hint to back away. Some did not understand what he was trying to do. After the picture, Maria started to walk away. Jeff had to think fast. "Wait, one more!" Jeff said as everyone started to gather into the frame. Jeff kicked behind him and waved with his right hand to indicate that he did not want them in the picture. He craved to take a picture alone with Maria. The others finally got the hint and backed away slowly as they giggled. Maria realized what Jeff was trying to do and was happy to take a picture alone with Jeff.

"OoooK, I see you, Jeff," Joel whispered as he backed away slowly. The other kids snickered.

Jeff cut Joel a side-eye and mouthed, "Shut up!" They all chuckled again.

Jeff waited until only he and Maria were on the screen, then he pressed the button. Jeff and Maria took one last picture, together, with great big smiles on their faces.

After all the guests left, Jeff, and parents cleaned the house and moved furniture back into place. Jeff did not have many words, but the delight on his face said it all. He could not stop smiling. Usually Jeff would be so focused on opening his gifts that his parents would have to plead with him to help clean up. Not this year! Jeff seemed to float around the house, still beaming from all of the fun he had with his new friends and his one very special guest. Mr. and Mrs. Whitman taught Jeff not to worry, but to *be* happy. Observing the smile on his face, confirmed how he was feeling.

Chapter 12

Jeff's New Squad

By all indications the ROT3 tournament was a great success. It was well attended, everyone who participated had a great time, and days later everyone who was there was still talking about it. However, Hines was consumed with Jeff's party. "Where did all of those other kids come from?" He thought. Hines was sure that all of the kids from their school (especially Jeff's friends) were at the ROT3 tourney. "How did Jeff have so many other friends?" Eaten up with these thoughts, Hines could not sleep. He had to know. Jeff had taken his best bud, Phil, from him. Phil attended the ROT3 tournament, which brought Hines great satisfaction, but Hines was not going to rest until he figured out who Jeff's new friends were.

Jeff was even more popular at math and science camp after his epic birthday bash. They teased him about Maria. Secretly, all of the boys thought Maria was the prettiest girl they had ever seen, but they never mentioned it to Jeff. Joel was still annoyed by the "Jeff Sucks" banner from the ROT3 tournament and was determined to get access to that game. Something did not feel quite right about it. He wanted to understand what all of the fuss was about. Joel texted his cousin Bryce to ask him about the game.

> Joel: Cuzzo, ROT3 tourney was lit! Saw when I was at Jeff's. Hook me up.
>
> Bryce: Wassupcuz! Yeah, it was dope. My download link expired. I will check with Hines. One sec.
>
> Bryce: Yo, Hines. My cousin wants link 2 ROT3. Send new link?
>
> Hines: Idk. Who is your cousin how did he hear about it?
>
> Bryce: He was at Jeff's party and saw the banners and stuff. He's cool!
>
> Hines: How does he know Jeff?
>
> Bryce: Dude, you askin too many questions! Jus send da link!
>
> Hines: OK. Cool. Send me his cell.
>
> Bryce: Cuzzo, U In. Hines will text you da link.
>
> Joel: OK. Cool! Hit me up 2morrow!

"*Yes!*" Joel and Hines were both excited shouting with excitement.

"This could be my way in. I can find out where all of those kids came from. Hines thought as he prepared to send the text to Joel.

"Yes Sir! All I need is access. I will figure out what dis dude is up to." Joel sat by his phone awaiting the link..

As soon as Joel received the link, he downloaded it onto his computer. Joel immediately tried to hack into the game. As he entered codes to access the backdoor, he was surprised to see that the game was not encrypted. There was a low-level firewall, but within seconds he was in. "Rookie!" Joel said.

At first glance, the code seemed standard. Joel did not see anything sinister. After a couple of hours of looking around, he decided to just play the game. The game required a headset with a mic. This enabled you to talk to others who were also playing the game. Joel created a player profile and waited for an invite to join an existing team. No one was inviting Joel to join his or her team because his username was unfamiliar. Your skill level, number of lives, and arsenal of weapons determined your value as a teammate. Teams invited individual players based on their ability to help them destroy the Big Bad Boss, Jeff. Finally, his cousin Bryce accepted Joel on his team.

Joel continued to play the game for hours. Joel did not really like the game but did not understand why he always had the urge to "keep going" and that he was "almost there." "Almost where?" he thought, a confused look on his face. Once he lost all of his lives, his cousin instructed him to say, "Jeff sucks!" until someone in the game gave him a life. "What? I'm not saying that. Just give me a life!"

"Dude! It's the rules." Bryce replied.

Joel did not want to look suspicious, so he said it. "Jeff sucks!" Joel repeated several times as his little brother barged into his room.

"What ya doing?"

"Something!" Joel answered.

"Can I play?" Joel's little brother asked as he looked over his shoulder and saw his computer screen.

"Not now, maybe later. But 'don't tell Jeff!'" Joel replied. "What! Why did I say that?" Joel asked as he shook his head back and forth, attempting to clear his mind.

Joel continued to play the game for a couple more hours until he fell asleep at his computer with his headphones still on. His team continued to play, and their every move seeped through Joel's headphones. "Jeff sucks...Jeff is the enemy...Don't tell Jeff!"

***

It was Monday morning, when Jeff arrived; he searched for Joel but found him already engaged with other students. Joel was typically standing by the door waiting for Jeff to arrive, but today was different. Jeff did not think anything of it; he simply joined in where Joel was sitting. Jeff attempted to make eye contact with

Joel so that he would not rudely interrupt what they were doing. However, when Jeff sat down, within a few seconds Joel left the group without greeting Jeff.

"That was strange," Jeff thought as his eyes followed Joel as he walked away.

Joel continued to avoid Jeff for the rest of the morning. To Jeff, this behavior was reminiscent of the conduct from his classmates at the Wheatland's. "Oh no! Not him too!" Jeff thought, worried. As the lunch period approached, Jeff decided that he would just walk up to Joel to ask if he had done anything to offend him, but when he walked toward Joel he sat at a table with only one open seat. Jeff walked by the table and made eye contact with Joel. Joel saw the sadness on his face as Jeff walked by. Jeff found a seat next to other students, but he could not help but wonder, "What's going on with Joel today?"

"Why did I do that?" Joel thought. Many thoughts raced through Joel's mind throughout the day: "Jeff sucks! Jeff is the enemy. Don't tell Jeff!" "Where is all of this coming from?" Joel thought.

The day ended, and as Joel rode home with his dad, he contemplated, "Why have I been thinking such bad things about my friend?" Joel paused, understanding dawning on him. "It must have been that dumb game!" That was the only thing that he had done out of his normal routine.

"Jeff is not my enemy! Jeff is cool! Jeff is my *friend*!" Joel declared out loud. His dad looked at him with a puzzled stare. Joel jumped out of the car and ran upstairs to his room. He tossed his backpack on the floor next to his desk and plopped down in his chair. He was determined to figure out why he felt that way after playing the game all night long.

Jeff was quiet on the way home from summer camp. Jeff's dad had not seen him look this sad since before his epic birthday bash. After they got home, Jeff's dad nudged his wife for her to look at Jeff as he walked through the kitchen. When she saw the look on Jeff's face and his body language, she asked, "What's up with him?"

"Not sure. He was not too talkative on the ride home."

Jeff's mom and dad were determined not to have another episode like before, so they devised a series of questions to determine what was on Jeff's mind. Just then Jeff's mom's phone rang. She saw it was Mrs. Brown, Joel's mother.

She answered.

> Mrs. Whitman: Hey Laurie!
>
> Joel: Hi, Mrs. Whitman. This is Joel. I hope you are having a wonderful day. Jeff is not answering his phone. Is he available?
>
> Mrs. Whitman: Oh. Um. I am so glad you called. Yes, he is. One sec—Jeff!
>
> Joel: Thank you so much.
>
> Jeff (from his room): Yes, Mom?

Mrs. Whitman: Telephone!

Jeff: For me? (Jeff ran toward the kitchen.)

Mrs. Whitman: Yes, it's Joel. He called on my phone. (She handed Jeff the phone.)

Jeff: What's up, Joel?

Joel jumped right in, the words spilling out of his mouth. "Jeff! You not gon' believe dis! I gotta hold of dat game and…"

"Wait, what? Slow down Homie! Am I on speaker?" Jeff interrupted.

"Yeah. OK, my bad! I knew there was somethin' shady with dat game, so…" Joel explained how he had schemed to get access to the game and how easy it was to hack into it.

Joel continued to explain his findings. Joel had sat at the game for a couple hours before calling Jeff. He still had not seen anything wacky, but while he was at math and science camp, his computer was still connected to the game. Hines had logged in during the day to update some of the code. Joel's computer was tracking Hines's every keystroke. Right before Hines logged out, he went to a file called "SweetRevenge." When Joel hacked into that file, he discovered the subliminal messages and the intervals at which they appeared during the game. It seemed as if Hines had recently increased the interval speeds so that the messages appeared more times per minute.

"You have never played the game, right?" Joel asked Jeff, wondering what effect the subliminal messages would have on him.

"No, I tried to play once, but it did not work.

"I can tell you what those messages said, but can you handle it?" Joel asked Jeff. Joel had written all of the messages down.

"Bro! He got hidden messages in the game that say, 'Play one more game,' 'You are almost there,' 'Playing indoors rules!' 'Don't tell Jeff,' 'Hines is cool,' and 'Jeff sucks!'

Joel felt relieved to understand why he had had those mean thoughts about his friend and even self-consciously avoided Jeff all day long. And I am so sorry for acting like a jerk today!" Joel apologized. "

"I knew it! That explains why all of a sudden my friends no longer wanted to play outside with me. I knew Redgrave was up to something, but who knew he was smart enough to think of something so clever." Though Jeff was angry, he was slightly impressed with Hines's scheme.

"Well, I think he has met his match," Joel countered, interlocking his fingers, twisting his wrists, and stretching his arms out in front of him. "I gotta plan! See if I can come through on Friday to tell you how we gon' get at dis fool.

"I will ask if you can sleep over so that we have more time to take him down," Jeff said with excitement.

***

Jeff and Joel wasted no time when Joel arrived. "What would you two like for dinner?" Jeff's mom asked as they blew past her on their way to Jeff's bedroom.

"Pizza please!" Jeff shouted before his bedroom door slammed shut.

"What are those two up to?" Mrs. Whitman wondered.

Joel pulled out a spiral notebook where he had written their goals for getting even with Redgrave. It listed the steps they would take to accomplish each goal, and the dates by which they would accomplish each step.

"We must have a strategy and perform each step in a specific order if we are going to be successful," Joel explained. Jeff was gazing at Joel's notebook but did not understand all that Joel had concocted. There were lots of numbers and formulas, so all the words ran together. Jeff had a new respect for Joel. He knew he was smart but had never seen him in action outside of summer camp.

"If all goes as planned, Hines will never know what hit 'em!" Joel concluded.

"OK, Joel, where do we start?"

Joel was already pecking away at his laptop, attempting to log into ROT3, when he realized he was not connected to Wi-Fi. "Jeff, what's your SSID and passcode?" Joel asked without looking up.

"My what?"

"Your Wi-Fi name and passcode." Joel used terms that would be more familiar to Jeff.

"The passcode is Super Pencil23!" Jeff replied. Joel was still typing at what looked like the speed of light to Jeff.

"Anytime now, Jeff. Wi-Fi code?" Joel asked again.

"I told you—Super Pencil23!" Jeff repeated. Joel stopped typing and looked up at Jeff.

"'Super Pencil'? What's so super about a pencil?"

"Oh yeah, with a capital *S* and capital *P*," Jeff said.

"Ugh! It's not working!" Joel exclaimed. "I don't know why I can't access the game. Yo, did yo parents pay da Internet bill?" Joel joked.

"Dad? Dad!" Jeff yelled a second time as his bedroom door swung open. "The Wi-Fi is not working. Can I access your work Wi-Fi, please?" Jeff pleaded.

"It's working, 'cause I am on it," Mr. Whitman replied. Jeff's dad sensed they were doing something important to them, so he just walked into Jeff's bedroom and to Joel's computer and typed in the password to his work Wi-Fi network.

"Be sure to forget the network before you leave," Jeff's dad instructed.

"Yes sir, Mr. Whitman!" Joel replied. Immediately, Joel was able to access the game. "Wait a minute." Joel stopped typing. "Yo dad was just on your Wi-Fi and it worked. But I could not access ROT3 from your Wi-Fi. As soon as we switched to yo dad's work Wi-Fi, I got it."

"What do you mean?" Jeff asked.

"Joel did some additional investigating on the Wi-Fi debacle. "This dude blocked yo IP Address from accessing the game. Have you even tried to download the game?"

"No. I never tried to download it."

"OMG! Jeff! You are not going to believe this! It appears that your Wi-Fi IP address was blocked from downloading the game! F*@#! Now I'm really pissed! Hines really had it out foyo a**!" Joel shouted.

"Hey! Watch your language! We don't use that kind of language in our home. Besides, my parents are down the hall," Jeff told Joel.

"Sorry, dude! I'm in! He's going down! Here we go!" Joel's fingers were flying fast as lighting across the keyboard.

"Super Pencil! That's it!" Jeff gasped.

"Here you go with this Super Pencil again," Joel said with a smirk.

Jeff had a revelation. Jeff rushed over to his desk drawer and pulled out a box. The box was black with metallic gold trim. Inside the box was an envelope that looked kind of thick. Jeff slowly pulled something out of the thick envelope. "Super Pencil" was emblazoned across the front of the book. The cover showed a muscular super hero standing on top of a building, overlooking a city with the sun shining brightly. He had a long red cap that flapped in the wind. It appeared that Jeff was moving in slow motion as he laid it in front of Joel. "This is how we will get back at Redgrave!" Jeff exclaimed.

Jeff and his dad finally finished writing their *Super Pencil* comic book. Without Jeff knowing, his dad sent his book to an editor and his mock-ups to an illustrator to finish the book. The editors were so excited about the storyline that they offered them a publishing deal. The new publisher sent them a copy of the book formatted for print.

"This is my best saga yet. When my friends read it, I know they will want it, they will love it and want to help Jeff save the world again!"

Jeff attempted to hand the book to Joel again. Joel continued to peck at the keyboard. The cover was so extremely vibrant that Joel did a double take after seeing Jeff's name out of the corner of his eye. "Wait, that says 'by Jeff Whitman.' Yo! Did you write dis?" The cover fascinated Joel. Joel stopped typing and reached for the comic book. Jeff pulled it back to his chest. "Look, but don't touch. You gotta wash your hands first!" Jeff cautioned.

"It's a comic book—I can't break it. Let me see!" Joel replied.

"But your greasy fingers can damage it!" Jeff fired back.

Joel took the book from Jeff. As he read and flipped through the pages, Joel marveled at the quality of the graphics. Before he knew it, Joel had been captivated by the comic book for several minutes. "You might be on to something, Jeff. How will we add *Super Pencil* to our strategy? " Joel passed the book back to Jeff and began typing on his computer again.

Chapter 13

The Big Payback

Jeff stood over Joel's shoulder and watched him type. Joel was explaining what he was doing as he went along, but he was using computer code terminology that Jeff did not understand. Jeff's eyes crossed when he attempted to follow along on the screen. The numbers and symbols on the screen looked like a different language to Jeff. After a while, Jeff plopped down on his bed, lay back, and waited for Joel to finish. "Just tell me when you are done," Jeff said with frustration.

"Almost there. I gotta hurry and close out before Hines logs back in."

That night, Hines was out with his parents. Hines received a sense of validation from monitoring the number of kids that downloaded and played his game. He frequently logged in to see how many kids were playing at any given time. He even had remote access through his Smartphone. However, his mother did not allow him to play on his Smartphone while they were at dinner or having family time. Hines did not particularly enjoy family time because his brother Luke always did things to annoy him. This night, Hines's mom had taken his device because she caught him trying to log into ROT3 while they were out at dinner. "You will get it back once we get home," Mrs. Redgrave said sternly after he disobeyed a third time. Hines was usually allowed to play with his phone in the car, so he asked for it as they left the restaurant, but today his mom was adamant due to his defiance of her rules at dinner. "No! You will get it when we get home. If you ask again, you will not have it for the entire weekend."

Joel was not aware of it, but Hines losing phone privileges allowed him the time he needed to rewrite the subliminal code within the video game. Joel also needed some extra time to mask the subliminal messages so that it was not obvious to Hines when he logged in. He duplicated Hines's "SweetRevenge" folder then disabled the real one. Next, he rewrote code that controlled the subliminal messaging. If Hines logged into his system, at first glance everything would look the same as how he left it. Joel encrypted the new subliminal message folder just in case Hines found it. Even if Hines found it, it would take him weeks to hack into the folder to discover what it was and what it was doing. Therefore, he would never suspect that his subliminal messages had been reprogrammed.

"OK, per the system log, on Fridays he typically checks his stats at ten fifty p.m. and the system does an auto scrub at eleven p.m., so we only have seventeen more minutes. Here is the plan." Joel began to explain in laymen's terms. Joel and Jeff brainstormed new subliminal messages that would not only reverse how the students subconsciously felt about Jeff, but would also spark an interest in reading *Super Pencil* with him.

"'Jeff is cool!' 'Jeff is our friend!' 'Let's save the world!' '*Super Pencil* is great!' 'Fun in the sun!' 'Let's be friends!'" Jeff rattled off, and Joel typed in the new subliminal messages to replace the old ones. Joel thought they were kind of lame, but he continued to type.

"I got one: Hines is a..." Joel blurted.

"Hey!" Jeff said, glaring at Joel.

"Oh yeah. Sorry! OK, how about 'Hines is a jerk'?" Joel suggested as he erased the bad name and typed 'JERK!' in capital letters.

Jeff paused and shook his head back and forth to signal what he was feeling inside. "No. Take it off."

Joel turned and looked at Jeff with a puzzled look. "What! This is your chance to get him back! You have to put something. Do you remember that banner? 'Jeff Sucks!' was plastered across the entire house for the world to see!" Joel said with disgust in his voice.

"I know, but erase it. I remember how it made me feel, so I don't even want Hines to experience that. I just want it to go back to how it used to be. Take it off!" Jeff commanded.

"You must be a saint or somethin'. If it were me, I would have cracked 'em over da head a long time ago. But if you say so." Joel turned to erase the insults.

Jeff continued to explain. "I will be just like him if I put bad things about him. I won't stoop that low."

"Ok. If you say so." Joel removed the derogatory messages about Hines as well as the good messages about Jeff. He finished typing the final coding, closed the file, and was working to activate the encryption. "Almost done...there!" Joel raised his arms in the air as a sign of victory, then glanced over at the clock.

At the same time, Hines sat at his computer to log in.

"Hines!" his mom called.

Hines turned away from this screen and looked toward his bedroom door as it opened. When he turned away, his screen flickered as the files updated and Joel exited his system.

"Here is your phone. Next time, I will keep it for the entire weekend. No computer! It's time for bed." His mom frowned and tossed his phone on the bed.

"OK, but I just need to do a system check first." Hines turned to his computer and followed his normal routine. Nothing appeared out of the ordinary, so he checked his stats, logged off, and got ready for bed.

***

Jeff and Joel read through the strategy Joel had created. Jeff added to the plan based on the notes he had taken over the past several months. Part of their plan was to get *Super Pencil* into the hands of all of their friends, but they did not know how to make it happen.

"Didn't you say your dad helped you with this book?" Joel asked.

"Yeah," Jeff replied.

"Let's ask him!" Joel suggested. The bedroom door opened. It startled Joel. It was Jeff's dad.

"What are you two up to?" he asked.

"Nothing!" they replied at the same time, sounding suspicious.

"Well, last call for snacks," Jeff's dad called back as he exited the room.

"Wow, don't anyone knock around here before bustin' in? Haven't they heard of privacy?" Joel asked, wide-eyed.

"Privacy! Tah! My dad says this is his house—I am only borrowing everything in it. So there are no locks on the doors, and they have the right to enter when they want. I get privacy when I move out and start paying for my own place," Jeff explained.

Joel had a puzzled look on his face, but he just followed Jeff to the kitchen for a late-night snack.

The next morning, Jeff woke up to the smell of bacon. Jeff nudged Joel as he ran to the bathroom to wash his hands and face. "Breakfast is ready. Hurry up before I eat it all!"

At breakfast, Jeff started to implement their strategy. "Dad, since we are finished with *Super Pencil*, I would like to send it to all of my old friends. You know, for old times' sake." Joel glanced at Jeff and thought it was ingenious how Jeff blended their plan into the conversation.

"That's a good idea, Jeff. I just need a list of your old friends and their contact information and I will make it happen," Jeff's dad replied.

"I have all of their contact information from Jeff's epic birthday bash list. We can use that," Jeff's mom chimed in. "Would you like us to include your friends from summer camp too?" Jeff's mom added, not wanting Joel to feel left out, but not realizing it was apart of his plan.

"Sure, Mom! That's cool," Jeff answered.

Chapter 14

A New School Year

A few weeks had passed since Joel made the backend adjustments to the ROT3 video game. Summer camp ended, and Jeff had returned from visiting his grandparents in Detroit. He was preparing for his first day of school.

"My son is going to middle school! Excited about a new school year?" Jeff's dad asked.

"Kinda," Jeff arranged outfits that matched his new shoes for every day of the week.

"That doesn't sound like your excited!" Jeff's dad replied. "Your schedule seems really cool. You have a couple male teachers for math and history. You have never had a male teacher before, right?"

"Yeah." Jeff was only giving one-word answers. His dad noticed.

"What's on your mind?" Jeff's dad asked.

"Actually, I am a little nervous about the start of a new school year. Last year, all of my friends stopped talking to me. I made new friends at summer camp, but they all go to different schools." Jeff paced the floor holding a shirt in each hand.

"I understand your concerns, son. You had the same concerns about summer camp and look at what happened. You are a cool kid. You are smart, funny, compassionate, and very friendly. Just be you. I am sure they will come around," Jeff's dad said encouragingly.

Jeff loved words of affirmation from his dad. He hugged his dad and then prepared to iron his clothes for the week; a routine that his parents started about a year prior.

***

It was a cool breezy morning. The sun was shining, and Jeff's shadow raced in front of him with each step he took. Jeff admired the colors of the leaves as he walked down the sidewalk, avoiding goose poop every two steps. His parents trailed him—close enough to provide some support but far enough away so Jeff would not feel like they were hovering. Once they got to the end of the block, they saw that a group of students was already waiting at the bus stop.

"Hi, Jeff!" one student called out.

"What's up, Jeff!" shouted a second classmate.

"Jeffster!" said another.

Many of the kids called out to him when they saw him. Jeff's eyes widened slightly. He was surprised to be greeted by so many classmates. Jeff quickly turned his head to make eye contact with his parents. The kids' greetings shocked him so much that he never actually responded.

"Hey, Jeff, my mom told me you had Mr. Woods for math?" Jacob said as he unfolded his schedule.

"Yeah," Jeff said as his stride matched Jacob's.

"Me too!" Jacob replied.

Jeff's parents stopped several houses back and watched Jeff interact with the other kids at the bus stop. They were delighted to see Jeff blend in so quickly. They peered from a distance as the kids boarded the bus, but Jeff never turned around to say goodbye. Jeff had not even noticed that his parents were no longer behind him. They smiled and turned to walk back home after watching Jeff sit down right before the bus pulled away.

Jeff had a great morning. He saw many new faces, and to his surprise, many of his friends from summer camp did attend his new middle school. He could not remember feeling like this while at school in a very long time. He spent time in the hallway between his first few classes mingling and catching up with old friends and new ones from summer camp.

At lunch, several of his classmates invited him to eat with them. Having the ability to choose whom to sit with was exhilarating for Jeff, but it was also overwhelming! Jeff did not want to say no to any of them, so he just gathered everyone and found a lunch table where they all could sit and eat together.

"Remember that summer when we all wore our Halloween costumes outside and pretended to save the world?" Jeff looked off into the distance, reminiscing.

"Oh yeah! I forgot all about that!" shouted one of the boys, as those same sentiments echoed around the table followed by a big laugh.

A student walked up to the table while they were laughing and addressed Jeff. "Jeff, I love your new comic book. Thanks for sending me a copy. My mom wants to order some for all of my cousins!"

"Oh yeah, thanks, Jeff!" The other kids affirmed. "It was fire!"

Their laughter was so loud that it got the attention of the other students who were eating in the cafeteria. As Hines and his crew entered, they heard the laughter coming from the tables that lined the window.

"Looks like Jeff and his friends are having fun. Lots of fun!" Billy said with an undertone of pleasure in his voice.

"Jeff and his friends?" Hines said as he scrutinized the faces at the table where Jeff was sitting. Hines could not believe his eyes.

"Why are these numbskulls talking to this lame-o again?" Hines sputtered under his breath. Hines and Jeff made eye contact. Hines had a snarling look on his face, but Jeff had a peaceful stare. Jeff waved. Hines was bewildered by the gesture. He looked to his left and right, and then behind him, to confirm that Jeff was waving at him. Hines then realized Jeff was waving at Billy.

"What are you smiling about and why are you waving at him?" Hines barked at Billy when he saw the smirk on his face. Billy quickly adjusted his demeanor, put his head down, and followed behind Hines. They walked across the room sat at the tables at the opposite wall from where Jeff and his squad were sitting.

Jeff shook his head slightly and rolled his eyes, but then quickly re-engaged in the conversation at his table so that no one noticed the exchange that had just taken place between him and Redgrave.

At their table across the room, Hines was fuming. "I just don't understand why they are talking to him again!"

"What do you mean? Everyone has always liked Jeff." Billy rebutted.

"What! I made sure that no one would ever talk to him again!" Hines blurted, and then he realized he had just let his secret slip out. "I mean…you know…never mind," Hines babbled. Hines continued to simmer as he gave Jeff the side-eye from across the room. Jeff never looked in his direction again but continued to enjoy lunch with his friends. Lunch period was almost over. Jeff cleaned his table, placed his tray on the conveyor belt, and exited the cafeteria on his way to his next class.

Hines left the cafeteria and went to the nurse's office. "I am not feeling very well," he told her.

"It must have been something you ate at lunch. Just lie right here for a little while, and we will see how you feel in a bit," suggested Mrs. Butler, the school nurse.

"I think I should just call my mom and go home. Gaggag!" Hines turned on the drama, trying to make himself regurgitate his lunch to increase the chances of Mrs. Butler believing his charade. It worked. Mrs. Butler called Mrs. Redgrave, but she was still at work so she sent Hines's brother, Luke, to pick him up from school.

Hines was not really sick. He just wanted to get home immediately to see what was wrong with his video game. As soon as Luke pulled into the driveway, Hines hopped out of the car and ran up to his room.

"By the way, I told Mom you were faking!" Luke exclaimed.

Hines spent hours investigating the coding of the game but could not find anything out of the ordinary. "Luke! Come look at this!" Hines shouted to his brother. "I need your help!"

"What do you want, you faker?" Luke said as he burst into Hines's room.

"Something is off about my game and I can't figure it out. Can you help me please?" Hines asked in an uncharacteristically nice tone.

The video game was a soft spot for Luke. Luke was actually extremely proud of the success that his little brother's game was having. Even some of his college friends played the game. "I taught him everything he knows," Luke would say to his friends whenever they said anything about the game.

"What am I looking for?" Luke asked.

"Just look please," Hines asked politely.

"But if I don't know what's wrong, I don't know where to look." Luke sat down at Hines's desk.

After about five minutes at the keyboard, Luke did not find anything "wrong." Joel had done a great job masking what he had done within the code.

"What is this 'SweetRevenge' folder?" Luke asked.

"Never mind! I'm good. I will take it from here!" Hines said as he rudely rushed his brother off the computer, pushing him aside. Hines did not want Luke to discover the hidden code within that folder.

"I was trying to help you, and this is the thanks I get?" Luke pounded random commands on the keyboard.

"Stop it!" Hines yelled as he shoved his brother again. Although Hines was a hefty kid, his brother was bigger. Therefore, the intensity of the push forced Hines backward and barely moved Luke. Annoyed and muttering to himself about fakers, Luke stormed out of Hines's room.

It was now early evening. Hines still sat at his computer, even more frustrated than when he had started. He stared at the screen, trying to decipher and undo the prompts that had resulted from Luke's banging. Just as he was finishing, his mother stormed into his room.

"Luke told me you were faking! Did you leave school early to play this silly video game?" Mrs. Redgrave shrieked.

"But, Mom…" Hines tried to chime in.

"I told you, I did not mind you doing this computer stuff as long as you took care of your other responsibilities. Since you can't handle it, I will take your computer until I feel you are ready." Mrs. Redgrave grabbed Hines's laptop from his desk and walked out the door. Luke walked past Hines' room with a grin on his face. Hines jumped up and slammed his bedroom door.

Hines understood that without that video game, he had no chance of stopping those kids from talking to Jeff. "I just don't understand what happened. 'Sweet Revenge' was mine."

Back to Normal

"Jeff, tell me about your first week of middle school," Jeff's dad said

"It was great! All of my friends are talking to me again, and some of my friends from math and science camp are in a few of my classes!"Jeff said as he took a shot on the miniature basketball rim that hung over his bedroom door.

"You seem very happy now that your friends are talking to you again. Why did that make you so sad before?" Jeff's dad asked, knowing the answer, but wanted Jeff to process his emotions about it.

Jeff always had to think really hard about his dad's questions. His dad would also allow long periods of silence while he waited for Jeff to answer. Jeff was uncomfortable, and the silence was awkward.

Jeff thought to himself, "In a few seconds, my dad is going to say, 'Still waiting!' so I better think of something fast. If I say, 'I don't know,' he is going to say, 'That is an unacceptable answer from anyone who has a brain.' Followed by, 'Don't say what you think I want to hear—just tell me what you are thinking.' But I don't know what I think...come on, Jeff, say something!"

"Still waiting!" Mr. Whitman caught the ball as it bounced off the rim. "Don't say what you think I want to hear. Just tell me what you think."

"You asked why it made me so sad that my friends were not talking to me?" Jeff repeated the question to buy himself a little more time.

"Yes, son." Mr. Whitman sank a shot from the hallway.

"Actually, I guess it is because I really like having friends around. I know you always say that I have a good imagination and I play well by myself, but it is more fun when others are around. When the people I care about stopped talking to me, it made me feel like something was wrong with me. I did not think I had done anything to them that would cause them not to like me. I felt very alone and like I had no friends. Seeing all of my new friends at my epic birthday bash helped me realize I did have more friends. Then this week, all of my old friends started to talk to me again. They even said that I was cool and that they missed how we used to save the world together."

"Son, the things that we experience in life should help us learn who we are and the types of people we are around. We will discover that not everyone is meant to be our friend. Everyone makes mistakes, so we should forgive people when they do make mistakes, but that does not mean that they have to become our best friends again. When someone shows you that they are not the type of person you can trust as a friend, believe their actions and not their words. We cannot control what other people say and do. The important part is that we learn and grow from our interactions with them, and then adjust to how we respond in the future. Jeff, you taught me to not treat all people badly because of how one person treated you. I love your caring and compassionate nature."

Jeff hugged his dad tightly and then went to his room.

The Saga Continues

"Hines? You have a package!" Hines's mother yelled up to him. It was normal for him to receive mail since he invented a top-rated video-game app. However, this package looked different. Hines carefully opened the box and could not believe his eyes.

"*Super Pencil* by Jeff Whitman," he read as he looked at the cover. Hines started to read the comic. The plot was epic, and the illustrations were captivating. This is actually a cool comic book. Frustrated and confused, Hines put the book down and slightly pulled the hair on the top of his head with both hands. "What is happening right now?

Hines had a flashback from earlier in the week. He had been watching Jeff interact with all of his old and new friends. He had even witnessed Billy and Phil talking to Jeff between classes. "It was all going accordingly as planned. What happened? Why did they start talking to him again? Think, Hines, think!" Hines pondered over the details of his week. Then it hit him.

Hines ran to his mom's room and found his laptop in the same place she always hid it when he was grounded. He quickly logged on and went to the "Sweet Revenge" folder. Everything looked fine. He continued to look around the code, and there he saw it, a second "Sweet Revenge" folder. When he tried to access it, he realized it was encrypted. He tried continuously, but he could not access the folder. "I have to open it to see what's in this folder!" Hines thought frantically. "Someone must have hacked into my system! But how?" Frustrated tears began to form in his eyes. "That bozo Jeff is not smart enough to do this! Who? How?" Hines was so aggravated and focused on accessing the video-game files that he did not hear the garage door open, his mother come into the house, or her announcing that she was home.

"Hines! I'm home!" his mother yelled for the third time. She began to search the house then proceeded upstairs to check his bedroom. As her foot landed on the bottom stair, Hines was startled by its familiar creak. He had to think quickly before she caught him in her room and on his computer. There was only one solution. "I gotta shut the entire game down!" Hines thought. "All of my work and all of my fans will be lost! But, if I keep it up, who knows what's in that folder!" Hines heard his mom's footsteps ascending the stairs. He quickly typed a direct message to all of the end users: "Temporarily out of service. We will be back soon." And then he typed in the kill code to shut the game down. He heard his mother reach the top of the stairs. He waited a few more seconds to ensure that the push notification went through, and then he slid the laptop back between the nightstand and the bed and ran into her bathroom and closed the door.

Flush! The sound of the flush frightened his mom.

"Whew! That was a big one," Hines said as he emerged from the bathroom.

"What are you doing in my bathroom?" Mrs. Redgrave asked, giving him a weird look.

"Luke would not give me privacy. Hi, Mom!" Hines said as he appeared to finish buckling his pants. After a quick hug, Hines strolled to his room and closed the door. He then ran to his bed, buried his head in his pillow, and let out a thunderous shout. "I'll be back, Jeff Whitman! Just wait— I will get revenge!"

The saga continues....

Made in the USA
Lexington, KY
20 July 2018